CW00972669

PENIC

3805910045698 9

In Time
of Plague

In Time
of Plague

Thomas Hinde

ROBERT HALE · LONDON

5 MAR 2008

© Thomas Hinde 2006
First published in Great Britain 2006

ISBN-10: 0-7090-8136-7
ISBN-13: 978-0-7090-8136-4

Robert Hale Limited
Clerkenwell House
Clerkenwell Green
London EC1R 0HT

The right of Thomas Hinde to be identified as
author of this work has been asserted by him
in accordance with the Copyright, Design and
Patents Act 1988

2 4 6 8 10 9 7 5 3 1

BARNSLEY LIBRARY SERVICE	
10045698	
Bertrams	28.02.08
	£18.99

Typeset in 11¾/15½pt Palatino
by Derek Doyle & Associates, Shaw Heath
Printed in Great Britain by St Edmundsbury Press
Bury St Edmunds, Suffolk
Bound by Woolnough Bookbinding Limited

CHAPTER ONE

ASSEMBLY

THERE they all sat, dotted about the village hall, gathered in protest. Though in fact nothing remotely like *all*, Mrs Lorna Furnival noted, looking left and right from her seat in the front row, then putting both hands on top of her walking stick and turning to survey the rows behind her. Twenty at most. Mrs Furnival snorted – she had a cold, harder to throw off now she was 73 – and turned to face the stage again. It had been her duty to sit here at the front, she considered, though even now she preferred not to have people behind her who might tickle her.

Her father, she remembered, would tickle the soles of her feet when he came back from wherever he'd been, smelling of cigar smoke. Little Lorna would draw up her feet as far as she could as if trying to get them inside herself where her father's big hands couldn't reach them. She had her father's nose, broad based, large and triangular in silhouette, suggesting the steel nose-pieces worn by men in armour. She had grey hair which she never treated with colouring muck.

'Welcome to this special village assembly,' Frederick Fisher, Chairman of the Parish Council, began from the stage. 'Good of so many of you to turn up' – Mrs Furnival surpressed a grunt – 'on this lovely spring evening. I need hardly tell you we're gathered here to consider the rejection of the final appeal against the County Road Plan.'

'Get on with it,' Lorna Furnival muttered, loud enough for the chairman to hesitate in case there had been an interruption. Fred Fisher was about five foot five inches tall with a small, pointed black beard. A bumptious little twerp, was the way Lorna would have described Chairman Fisher. Believing he ran the village! Thinking he was well liked! What Fred Fisher liked was the sound of his own voice. If Lorna had ever troubled to assemble a case against democracy she would have considered Fred Fisher all the evidence needed. 'His heart's in the right place,' someone had once assured her. 'His what?' Lorna had replied.

It was on occasions like this that Lorna most missed her husband, Harry Furnival. Harry had also liked the sound of his own voice but she'd minded less, even wondered if in some way she encouraged him. Certainly she'd sometimes been proud of him, with the sort of qualifications a mother has about a successful child. 'Was that OK?' he'd ask afterwards. 'Not bad,' she'd say, because one shouldn't let a child get too pleased with himself. Though tonight she might have been kinder because his fondness for the village was genuine, as well as something they shared. On summer evenings they'd stand together on the back lawn, looking out across the treetops of their private wood to the downs far away on the horizon and seem to share a sense of wonder at their good luck.

Luck it had been when they'd been searching the Home Counties for an escape from London and a friend's friend had reported the 'For Sale' board. As soon as they had seen the house they'd known, and within a couple of months had arrived. That was more than forty years ago. The distant roar of jets reversing their engines, the unending moan of their nearest motorways, the concrete and slate terrace of council houses, these had come later.

Twenty years ago, Harry had left her. Still the early days of motorways when drivers of low cars who failed to realize that the juggernaut in front of them was braking could end up under its rear end, beheaded. Harry's new Jaguar – oh yes, another toy – had been just low enough.

'I've arranged to have the latest plans displayed . . .' Chairman Fred Fisher continued.

Typical, Lorna Furnival thought, to manage to suggest he had a minion or two to carry out his orders. Arriving punctually, she'd seen him busy with the drawing pins.

Others present had more principled objections to the chairman, in particular Mr Boon. Ernest Boon, early retired civil servant, perhaps forcibly retired, no one was sure, shared, in modified form, the outrage of his wife, Tiffany, not present, that Fred Fisher should unashamedly bring his mistress to church with him. Disgusting. Tiffany had even seen them holding hands at the communion rail. Though Tiffany was as short as Fred Fisher and slighter in build, she was fiercer. Wasp-like, some who sympathized with Ernest would say. Once she had been a nurse; Chairman Fred, in frolicsome mood, would say the Boons had met over a bed pan. In Tiffany's opinion the chairman was a stuck up little popinjay. She wasn't sure what a popinjay was, but pictured a blend of cock pheasant and Sir Walter Raleigh, whose portrait had hung in her parents' dining-room. Mincing about the stage! The chairman invariably played the lead – once juvenile, now less so – in village plays. It was Tiffany's disapproval of the chairman which had prevented her coming to this special assembly, but she'd needed to know what happened. 'You go and find out,' she'd told Ernest, actually quivering with fury, he'd observed, at the thought of the chairman's immorality.

The Boons had lived in the village almost as long as Lorna Furnival. For many years Ernest had commuted on the 7.34, before an office promotion enabled him to catch the 7.56. It was their passion for birds which had brought them here, where Tiffany's passion had declined – revealed as a ploy, Ernest suspected – while his own had grown, mixed with sickening regret at the disappearance of common species.

Twenty years ago he would be woken in the early hours, properly dark then, by nightingales loud outside his window. Then there had been yellow hammers in the lanes, coal tits and sometimes willow or marsh tits on his bird table, redwings and siskins in winter, even the occasional tree creeper secretively scaling the far side of the trunk of his flowering cherry, while down in the valley he had often seen kingfishers by Mrs Furnival's ponds. On summer evenings swallows would fill the sky, or if rain threatened skim the ground for insects. How few of them there were now. As for larks, once he'd read in his old school magazine the reminiscences of a boy who, fifty years before, had set out to walk home at the end of the summer term: '*How well I remember passing Silbury Hill at about six in the morning, with the larks high in the sky and the mowers already at work in the meadow*'. His sadness for this lost world would sometimes make his eyes water. In moments of despair he felt that instead of this death by attrition he would prefer annihilation at a single blow by suburbia which, for the past four years, had seemed increasingly inevitable. Meanwhile it was starlings and magpies that survived – and *cats*. These roused Ernest Boon to an anger almost as fierce as Tiffany's fury with the chairman. Once he had daringly driven his Morris 1000 Traveller at a killer tabby slinking across the road, missed it and grazed the wall of the Red Lion car-park, so leaving behind some of the car's half-timbering.

He and Tiffany lived at Meadowsweet, a diminutive cottage which seemed appropriate to their size – Ernest was also short, though fleshy – just as Lorna's mansion seemed right for her statuesque build. Tonight Ernest sat near her, also in the front row but separated by one unoccupied stacking chair, collecting examples of the chairman's deceitful speechifying to report to Tiffany and provoke her into the sort of anger he felt himself, but was too timid to express.

His attempted cat assassination must have occurred at about the time he had fancied Lorna. Perhaps there had been a connection. He still admired her, and now, hearing her impatient mutterings, was reminded why. She was defiantly herself. Perhaps he admired powerful women in general, even those as different as Lorna and Tiffany. The cackle of an alarmed blackbird in the bushes outside distracted him, taking him back to his childhood, fifty-five years ago, when his father would read to him on summer evenings – *Treasure Island*, *Masterman Ready*, *Dog Crusoe*. Ernest Boon had a round head and white hair which formed owl-like tufts above each ear, suggesting some child's toy, its face painted with a permanent expression of astonishment.

'Vell, if you ask me,' Mrs Volga said.

The whole assembly, all twenty of them, stirred in dismay, though their sighs were more an expression of relief that, acting together, they had for once the boldness to be openly rude. Lorna Furnival was not one of them. She might laugh at Mrs Volga but liked the way she didn't care what people thought of her.

'Yes, Vera?' Chairman Fisher said, polite but with a mocking smirk.

'It is not important,' Mrs Volga said, showing that although she seemed superficially to have the hide of an elephant she could sometimes be coyly sensitive. In fact she was always sensitive, but enjoyed being provocative, or indeed arousing emotion of any sort. Living in England, as she had done since her father escaped with her from Moscow, aged fifteen, was like swimming in tepid custard – urgh, horrid, but amusing. Mrs Volga, correctly Mrs Smithson, born Vera Toffsky, subsequently married to one Stanley Smithson, who had long ago fled from her, was short but broad.

Ernest Boon had once seen her bathing naked at the local Trades Union Recreation Centre and been amazed by the size of her mottled purple thighs. Chairman Fred Fisher, landing at Moscow Airport on his way to Tokyo – supposedly a trip in search of a Japanese hamlet to become the village's twin, in fact a little holiday he'd awarded himself after being shown some arousing Japanese postcards – had looked out of the plane's window and seen at least fifteen Mrs Volgas, identically five foot tall and uniformed in white, each with a huge brooms, sweeping the snow from the runways.

Mrs Volga lived at the north end of the village where the ground first began to dip towards the valley, this becoming deep and wooded below Lorna's property, in a neo-colonial bungalow, roofed with two-foot-square asbestos tiles set diagonally above grey, pre-fab walls. Inside, since there was little space, she slept on the top tier of a bunk bed, though it was a wonder to people who visited her how she managed to climb up. On the lower bunk she stored jars and saucepans, some of them containing part eaten meals, judging by the bungalow's ripe smell. Since she had no fridge she kept other food outside her back door under gauze cages weighted down with bricks to frustrate foxes. Few people, in fact, visited her, and it was perhaps because of this that Lorna Furnival occasionally did, and would accept a neat gin in a rather smeary glass.

'If you have anything to say . . .' the Chairman continued, hoping to exploit his success with his audience, but sensing that he might be losing support.

'I say, if poor people are needing houses, why are we not velcoming them? Now, I am shutting my mouth . . .'

That was better. All were united in relief.

'Hear hear,' Admiral Hawker said, referring to Mrs Volga's agreement to go about. Admiral Jack Hawker also sat in the front row since he was hard of hearing, his walking stick planted in front of him, both swollen hands planted on top of it – swollen not by seawater but from fishing. Coarse fishing. In any weather, wearing no gloves, he would bait his hooks, puncturing each squirming worm three times, the point ending at its anus, then sit for hours on a shooting stick waiting for the thrilling moment when his float gave its first bob. All this despite lumbago, which explained why he seemed to be stuck in this forward tilted position, knowing that leaning back would cause an agonizing spasm. Beside him his wife, Lady Anne Hawker, sat at a similar angle, propped by a similar stick. Without looking at each other they began a conversation.

'That woman!' Lady Anne.

Grunt. Admiral Jack.

'Should have been strangled at birth.'

'Her girth?'

'No, birth. Strangled.'

'Mangled?'

'Jack, you're crazy. All right, mangled.'

The admiral and his wife had settled in the village seven years ago on his retirement from his last command, a shore-training establishment HMS *Beehive*. That had not been a happy appointment for either of them. Aboard ship the admiral had been surrounded by things and people, all male, whom he understood. Custom and obedience ruled. Ashore, all kinds of confusing people – civil contractors, uncivil lady politicians – had asked questions and required decisions which muddled him. Nor was Anne Hawker pleased to have her husband's permanent company, forcing her to discover something she had hidden from herself for many years: how incompetent he was. She'd tried to help him, but this had taken the form of accompanying him on his rounds with a list of things he must not forget to do, a routine which made cadets snigger. In the evening Jack would read the *Express*.

'You're snoring, Jack.'

'Rubbish.'

'Wake up there.'

'Can't a fellow be tired?'

Their modest village house, thatched and weather-boarded, sited a hundred yards beyond Mrs Volga's shack, had been a haven. Here they had grown tolerant again, even fond of each other. Lady Anne had run the village Girl Guides, raised funds for the local town's hospice and grown tea roses. She and Lorna Furnival had for a time each been suspicious of another person who liked to say things which would shock. It was the County Road Plan which had made them allies, though Anne Hawker still considered Lorna idle while Lorna thought Anne much too busy. Meanwhile

Admiral Jack continued to fish for tench in Lorna Furnival's stream and black ponds, though more often now came home leaving his float, hook and worm dangling from the branches of a willow. The peace down there was almost as satisfactory as being at sea, a rare pleasure in his later years of service because of the price of fuel oil and the stinginess of left-wing ministers. Quietly, and tunelessly, he would start to hum, unaware that he was sometimes being observed through binoculars by Ernest Boon, crouched among nearby scrub as he watched for winter migrants.

Immediately behind the Hawkers sat their 27-year-old daughter, Briony, the name chosen by her mother whose spelling had never been good, the admiral being at sea at the time. While Jack and Anne Hawker were both tall and gaunt, Briony was short and massive. Once the admiral had had a dream – never confessed to his wife – in which Briony had suffered from a rare disease that made her keep swelling. He and Anne had stood outside her bedroom door, not daring to open it for fear of what they would find, though they could hear Briony inside there screaming for help. It was generally realizd that Briony's formidable width had frightened away possible boyfriends.

They had also perhaps been put off by her upper-class vowels. A group of the children of Mrs Prone, who lived in one of those post-war council houses which topped the ridge above the village and so distressed Lorna Furnival, would sometimes lurk in the long grass outside the Hawkers' privet hedge and when they saw Briony stump into the garden would call out 'Mummee', in a surprisingly good imitation of her Benenden accent.

Benenden had revealed that Briony had other problems, one of which her parents had been forced to recognize: that not only was she two-thirds their height and twice their width, but it was from her father, not her mother, that she had inherited her brains. A total of four O-levels, one of them in domestic science, had forced them to accept that asking her to attempt more, let alone any A-levels, would have resulted in more painful humiliations. Briony was now taking evening classes in typing, book-keeping and information technology, the latter sometimes making her hoot with laughter that anyone should expect her to understand it.

She had yet another problem which her parents were *not* aware of: Briony was in love, and the person she loved was Sandra. Sometimes she thought that if she ever dared talk to Sandra she would ask to be allowed to call her Sappho. She had little idea who Sappho was, but the name had caught her fancy when she first heard it whispered in Middle Dormitory.

But Sandra had a partner: Bob. Sandra and Bob Brandish lived in what had once been a caravan, but was now better described as a hovel in the trees at the bottom of Lorna Furnival's wood, where it had developed a green patina that thrived on the miasma rising nightly from the ponds close by. 'Got to live somewhere,' Lorna would growl if anyone asked her why she had lent it to them, though the only person who ever dared to be so frank was Mrs Volga. Sandra and Bob both had shoulder-length hair which hung down their necks in tight little curls and was probably similarly straw-coloured when washed.

They had produced a child, accidentally and irresponsibly most considered, now eight months old, named Foxglove. What they had done with Foxglove this evening it was difficult to imagine. Instead they had brought Truffle, a hairy whippet. For the occasion Truffle wore a muzzle, but this did not prevent him snarling at anyone who pushed past him where he crouched underneath their legs at the back of the hall. Here Sandra sniffed and Bob fingered the silver ring which he wore in his nose. 'Farming your line?' Chairman Fisher had once wittily asked him.

No one knew where Sandra had come from, though most guessed from another caravan. Bob's background they knew well: he was the son of the Chairman of the County Council, Sir Rupert Brandish – much to Sir Rupert's despair.

'*We* pay for them,' Lady Anne Hawker would say, referring to the pair and what she called their goings on.

'Always civil to me,' Admiral Jack Hawker would say. Bob Brandish had once supplied him with a tin of excellent maggots.

When not attending her secretarial classes, Briony Hawker would take lonely walks through the meadows which lay across the stream below Lorna Furnival's wood, hoping for a glimpse of Sandra.

But in these meadows she more often saw Gertie Jones, putting her seventeen-hand gelding, Tobias, over jumps in the next-door field. Gertie Jones was in love with Tobias. She would pat him – more accurately thump him, since she understood how horses felt – then nuzzle her weather-reddened face into his neck fur. The love Gertie might have felt for fellow humans had become directed during her upbringing in an orphanage, managed by Miss Lush, to horses, especially strong, simple and naughty ones. Few knew of her orphanage background, but many knew that she had subsequently wanted to be a policewoman, then, when rejected, a lorry driver, but had failed to acquire an HGV licence. It was rumoured that she had demolished a sixteen-wheel, thirty-eight tonner in the attempt, while others said she had given her instructor a nervous breakdown.

15

A couple of years earlier, Admiral Hawker, watching Gertie put Tobias at a hedge, had seen them come apart.

'Whoopsie!' the admiral said, rising from his shooting stick but not sure what to do because he was the wrong side of Lorna's stream.

'I say,' he shouted, as loudly as he could, in the hope that there was someone near who could go to the rescue, though there didn't seem to be.

Then, as he later reported to his wife, 'Blow me if she didn't come sailing back in the other direction. Must have remounted where I couldn't see 'em.' They'd sat thinking about it. 'Quite a girl, that one,' the admiral said.

Part of Gertie's problem was her eyesight. Recently, Tobias had placed a hoof on her thick-lensed, blue-plastic-framed glasses crushing them into the mud, with the result that all beyond the back of the chair in front of her was a blur. 'Oh hallo,' she'd shouted tonight, with a yelp of laughter, mistaking the admiral's wife for the admiral as she was wearing the deer stalker they both used. Gertie sat at the centre of the assembly, a mound of army-surplus camouflage jacket.

Tobias was in fact only five-eighths her property. She was paying for him in instalments. 'That's for his near fore,' she'd told the Witch of Finglethorp, local aristocratic horse dealer, as she'd handed over her latest payment. It was the threat to Tobias's way of life which the County Road Plan represented that had brought Gertie Jones here tonight.

'First the minutes of our last meeting,' Chairman Fred Fisher announced. 'Then I'll report subsequent developments.'

Virginia Ranch, Clerk to the Parish Council, began to read. 'The chairman reported that we had won second prize in the Tidy Village Competition. A motion to attach a commemorative plaque to the churchyard wall received three votes in support, three against, with one abstention. Mr Fisher, as chairman, gave his casting vote in favour.'

The chairman was rather short, Virginia admitted, but his thing was the opposite. She still shuddered when she recalled the first time she'd seen the chairman's thing. It had happened a year ago, after a particularly exciting parish council meeting at which two villagers had complained of the defeatest stance the parish council was adopting towards The Road Plan, when he, Fred, had been so witty and so crushing. They both lived in Chestnut Lane and at first Virginia hadn't understood what was happening as they walked home together and he began to edge her off the path into the fringe of Gullies Wood. 'Be careful, look out,' he kept saying, as he pushed her between tree trunks, using his hands on each side of her waist, where they presently began to tickle her.

'Oh Mr Fisher,' she'd had time to cry, before he engulfed her – that was how she thought of it – and they started a long, hugging, swaying kiss during which his tongue reached places where no one else's had ever before been, certainly not her husband, Michael Ranch's. Separated at last, they had stood gasping and staring into each other's eyes, though not for long. It was too cold and prickly for much undressing, but he had pushed her to the ground, thrown up her skirt and with thrilling impatience actually ripped her panties in removing them: that had been another first. It was then that she had seen it, swaying above her in the early spring dusk. She remembered it as dark red, almost black.

Wonderfully frightening as the next few moments had been, what subsequently gave her more secret happiness was that she'd been capable of such a reckless, indeed rather grubby, surrender. Because she knew that she was seen, even laughed at, as an exceptionally clean, properly behaved person, who never emerged from her bungalow without peach make-up and hair so firmly set that it seemed like a golden helmet. For this reason, even if she and Fred occasionally held hands, she was still able to think it impossible that anyone could believe them more than professional comrades, which was how Fred Fisher had once described their intimacy.

Michael Ranch knew better, of course, but he had been very sensible about it. Sometimes Virginia wished that her husband would be less sensible. A little outrage would have been more flattering. But the truth was that Michael Ranch, as cuckold, felt less outrage than relief, wishing Frederick Fisher luck in any attempt he might make to stir his wife to orgasm, something he'd failed to do and, though he was fond of Virginia, suspected to be impossible. Fred's wife, Wendy, had also been sensible, even quietly amused, telling herself, and occasionally a friend, that Virginia Ranch was an appropriate fate for Fred, the old stoat. Both Michael Ranch and Wendy Fisher had chosen not to attend the assembly and were at that moment sitting in their respective front rooms, watching the third or fourth repeat of an episode of *Dad's Army*. Presently, Michael Ranch, a tall, thin welfare officer with long pale fingers, went to help himself to some lentil soup – no eating of bloody flesh allowed in Virginia's home – and Wendy Fisher, a well rounded mother, went to wake her fifth child for a bedtime piddle.

At the special assembly the attention of many drifted as Virginia Ranch read on, so that several failed to raise their hands in approval when she stopped and there was a moment's silence, as if they were annoyed at the way their wandering thoughts had been interrupted. Miss Wiggum, headmistress of the village primary school, was thinking about the inspector. Six months had passed since his visit. 'A little old-fashioned,' he'd told her, when pressed for a general comment, and smiled condescendingly. Her huge bosom heaved with indignation when she remembered it. He was young enough to be her child. He'd been wearing *fur-lined bootees*.

Miss Wiggum had had charge of the village school for almost twenty years, during which she and the village had fought two attempts to close it, while its numbers had fallen from about fifty to under thirty.

Next to Miss Wiggum sat Ralph Gamble, moustached, with droopy purple-veined cheeks, these together suggesting a sad dog. Ralph was the organizer of the local shooting syndicate for which he bred pheasants. He was treated by some with respect, as the nearest thing to a squire they had. He'd been first to employ Gertie Jones in his garden and was amused to watch her fiercely, but somewhat indiscriminately, attacking weeds and perennials. Because he enjoyed exercising patronage he also rented her a room in one of the cottages he owned in the village street. He lived beyond Lorna Furnival, to the south of the village, on the site of what had indeed been the manor house, until his father pulled it down and replaced it with a magnificent Tudor mansion.

Ralph Gamble remembered all too well the first news he'd had of the County Road Plan, how he'd skimmed through the article with only superficial interest, until, there, second line of the third paragraph, he'd read the name of the village. Even then for some seconds he hadn't believed it. Somewhere else, of course, which by coincidence had the same name. His shock at discovering that it was indeed their village still made him sweat into his sideburns. 'Ultimately to provide access to new housing for approximately 50,000,' he'd read.

Just now, however, he was thinking more of the inadequate gratitude which Irma, his resident Swedish *au pair*, had shown for the Range Rover he'd recently bought her, not realizing that it was the way he ground his teeth at night, depriving her of the sleep she needed to remain beautiful, which made her irritable. While she, still not knowing how the English were all taught from birth to hide their feelings, seldom realized she was annoying him. This she would have preferred not to do, knowing that the buttering of her bread on the right side, as her phrase book put it, was important.

Irma Svenson had arrived in England a year and a half ago as an *au pair* for another member of the shooting syndicate, but after her memorable appearance one day as a beater, with pretty bare arms and a feather in her Swedish hunting cap, she'd been poached by Ralph. A month later he'd astonished himself by asking her if she'd like to drop by some time. Irma well remembered that occasion too, though less emotionally than Ralph, when she'd decided that beggars could not be choosers. By then her current employer, noticing her winks and Ralph Gamble's flushes, had already given her the bag.

Next to Ralph Gamble, sat Mrs Prone, compelling him to ease himself on to the opposing edge of his seat. Hers was Number 2 in that terrace of council houses which looked down on the village, named by a young housing officer in his early, optimistic days, Keats Villas. Mrs Prone's seven children had various fathers. Presumably some were by Jimmy Green, but when she'd last heard of Jimmy he was doing time for robbery with violence, the best place for him. Although she hoped he was still safely there, she never answered a knock on her front door without checking who was on the doorstep from her toilet window. Currently it would often be Billy Snipe.

'Open to all callers,' Chairman Fred Fisher sometimes remarked, about Shirley Prone. 'She should be fair wore out,' others would say, noticing with satisfaction her skinniness, but annoyed by her perennial appeal. Many in the village metaphorically turned their backs on what took place at Number 2, but this didn't prevent them sharing an enjoyable sense of outrage. Fancy the council building them up there, against the skyline for all to see. But what would you expect, some would say, confident that there must be some illegal connection. Tonight Shirley had come to the assembly guessing that her presence would confuse many of those who would be here, considering she was not the sort of person whose support they needed.

Two to her left sat Geoff Riddle, a mixed farmer – 'mixed up', Fred Fisher would say – from higher up the valley. He was thinking about a piglet. This annoying creature had escaped while he was trying to crate half-a-dozen weaners. Geoff and his labourer, Pike, had spent an hour hunting for it in the farmyard, not an easy task since this contained a mouldering haystack, three pick-up trucks with flat tyres, half-a-dozen piles of gates, wire netting and fencing posts, a chain harrow disappearing into lank grass, a dozen moulting hens and a donkey named Moses. 'Last of a dying breed,' Fred Fisher would say. 'Surviving by binder twine and prayer.' The piglet had taken shelter in an overturned milk churn and Geoff and Pike had stood there, bending in turn to peer in, then standing back to roar with laughter. Remembering it now, Geoff began to laugh again until he noticed the look Lady Hawker was giving him. In his mid-thirties, Geoff Riddle was tall and would have been handsome but for an alarming squint, the result, it was said of a frolic at agricultural college which had also made necessary a steel plate in his skull. 'To keep his brains in, those which hadn't already escaped,' some said. Others thought it might have been caused by a parting blow from his wife when she left him some years ago, and gradually this had become the accepted version, not because of better evidence but because it seemed appropriate. Living with Geoff day in day out, they would say! What would you expect?

Also present was Joan Wodge, wife of Wilfred Wodge, landlord of the Red Lion, a woman so short that her head alone would be visible as she passed to and fro behind the bar. Wilfred had sent her to spy on the meeting. He might have been expected to favour the Road Plan, which could bring him business, but his mind was so set in a mould of pessimism that he found looking forward hopefully to *anything* was not possible. Furthermore, he was certain that it was all a plot to raise his hopes then kick him in the teeth. And just supposing it did mean more trade, think of the extra work this would mean. He might – horrible thought – need to employ someone who would have to be paid and, God forbid, humoured. At present it was Joan who did any work which was done at the Red Lion, and this was not much since Wilf Wodge had only lately begun to offer any kind of food – white bread and cheddar sandwiches – and wouldn't look in the eye customers who asked for lager while holding out his hand for instant payment.

It was assumed that Wilf Wodge beat his wife, but if so Joan never complained. As for tonight's meeting, she'd been looking forward to it for days, had come wearing a straw sun hat with a band of artificial daises and now grinned so widely at anyone whose eye she caught that some believed a joke must be occurring behind them, others that their flies were undone.

Near, but not too near, to Joan Wodge sat Evan Mullins, a fellow tradesman until he closed his shop. Often in the morning he could now be seen at an upper window staring malevolently down on the young wives of the village as they swept by in their bright little cars on their seven-mile journey to the nearest supermarket, or still more viciously, because they were less of a moving target, at the older village women standing in the queue for the daily bus which would take them to the same place. These, looking up apprehensively at him, would see him muttering what they took to be Welsh curses, though in fact he wasn't making a sound. It was they who had ruined him. As for the Road Plan, he secretly welcomed this, which might once have made him rich, since it would confirm that God had always meant to punish him. So, though he pretended to oppose it, this was only to be able to laugh at them when God punished them.

Evan Mullins also disliked Fred Fisher, since it had been reported to him that Fred had proposed, when his shop was about to close, that a fund be started for buying it, complete with dusty tins of sardines, feather cobweb brushes and packets of soggy potato crisps, for preservation as a museum. 'Surely we should do something to save these relics of our past,' he would argue, and wait for someone to protest, so that he could wink at them to show he was joking.

Mullins's anger with those two lazy buggers down in the woods was even greater. One night, when the shop had finally closed and its dustbins were filled with tinned food so out dated that no one would buy it, he'd found them rumaging up to their elbows among it. So now they wanted what they wouldn't touch when they had to pay for it. Secretly he'd hoped they might poison themselves, and even punctured several tins to promote decay.

At last Fred Fisher reached 'recent events'. He didn't like to boast, but in the few days since the rejection of the final appeal against the County Road Plan he'd not been idle. He'd written another, even stronger letter to their local Member of Parliament – murmurs of contempt – and included copies of his seven previous letters.

'Yes, I know some of you feel we aren't as well served as we should be by this gentleman, but we must make the best of what God has given us' – murmurs of protest from the few regular church goers. 'Furthermore, I have sent copies of this whole correspondence to the Prime Minister, the Council for the Protection of Rural England, the RSPOB, the Southern Anglers Association. In the next few days I shall be considering the merits of establishing a separate Village Defence Committee, specifically concerned with our cause.'

'Didn't you tell us that like last time?'

A pause while the Chairman examined papers on his table, turning some to look at their backs, until the silence became embarrassing, then he continued as if no one had spoken. Now he reached his peroration, which he pretended not to need to glance down to read.

'People sometimes speak of local democracy. Then they allow this to happen. We may be a small, some would say an insignificantly small, community, but we must prove that, tiny as we are, we represent something of real, not to say universal importance: the right of everyone to live their lives in peace. We have won before' – he referred to those defeated attempts to close their school. 'With your help we shall win again.' He paused, but if hoping for applause was disappointed.

'Well now, do any of you have suggestions? The more the merrier.'

'We could lie down in the road,' Gertie Jones shouted. A worrying proposal as apart from the problem that the road didn't yet exist, some wondered which of them would lie down first, while others whether, once down, they would be able to get up again.

'You won't catch me . . .' Ralph Gamble began. 'If they come near my land. . . .' Ralph rarely finished a sentence, as if the moment he heard himself speak, such a lapse into intellectualism shocked him into silence. Now he raised his hands in front of him to sweep the ceiling of the village hall with an imaginary shotgun as he tracked an imaginary pheasant, so embarrassing those who recognized a threat he would never carry out.

'In my country,' Mrs Volga began, 'there is no unemployment . . .' These were Iron Curtain times.

Groans.

Now Bob Brandish was speaking, but in such a low mutter, his head so low the ring in his nose was only a few inches above his knees, that only those close to him could hear and some thought he was talking to his ugly dog.

'. . They're round like, yer know, with spikes like, yer know . . .'

Gradually it became clear that he was offering to manufacture iron balls of the sort used by Ancient Britons against Roman cavalry, each with four spikes, so spaced that one of them was bound to stick up vertically. As his meaning became clear he spoke into an increasingly hostile silence. 'You shits,' Sandra thought beside him, but Gertie Jones looked left and right, wide-eyed, cheeks puffed, as if wanting confirmation that anyone could suggest injuring horses in this way.

'Well, Bob, we could certainly keep some of those in reserve,' the chairman said merrily.

Eventually there were no more suggestions and all that could be heard was Admiral Hawker clearing his throat and an occasional snort from Lorna Furnival, this so exciting Ernest Boon sitting one seat away that he wished he had the courage to applaud.

Then Mrs Langridge spoke. 'Waarl . . .' Polly Langridge used the accent half the village had used when Lorna had arrived forty years ago. Beside her sat her husband, Sam, a strong and well-liked man of few words who used once to check the sewage plant in the valley until a county sewage officer was appointed. Every morning he would be seen walking down Bristle Lane, his responsibility giving him a certain dignity. Today, demoted, he would come at dawn with bucket and mop to clean the village's public toilet, these seeming a further insult because of the difficulty he had in carrying them, since his toes pointed outwards at an angle which made his two feet, if he ever stood to attention, almost form a single line. He was said to have been dropped when a baby, though no one explained how such an accident could have produced this malformation. Almost equally miraculous was the well-established fact that, when the village had had a cricket team, he had been its fast bowler. Though Sam was only forty six, for some forgotten reason he was known as Old Walnut. The Langridges had two sons, the eldest doing a thesis on Insect Phobias at Strathclyde University. 'Well blow me,' Polly would say proudly. 'No comment,' Sam would mutter.

'It's lark this,' Polly Langridge began, 'we 'as our differings but that don't make no matter . . .' Polly knew many things about the people of the village, some accurate, some less so. About the chairman she was especially well informed. Young Fred, she would tell, had arrived in the village as a pretty lad of 16, to help on the Riddle Farm and board with Professor Borthwick, a retired academic. Borthwick, known as Bobo, had for years been spending his holidays on the farm where he would hand milk the cows, before machines did it, and eye the comely farm lads. None had been so comely as Fred – this was before he grew his little black beard. In the evenings Fred was said to help Bobo with his research. 'What be they researchin'?' Polly would ask, with a huge wink. Homosexuality had been a recent discovery for her, and she spoke about it as if unsure whether or not people were teasing her.

Now she wanted to speak for them all, because they were really all good friends with each other, yes, even Mrs Volga they realized she was implying, and needn't feel ashamed of the comic things they often said of each other 'Well, don't it make us characters like, and ain't that better than being nobodies?' Some began to look around the hall and exchange smiles.

'Mrs Langridge,' the chairman said, and paused histrionically, 'no, I'm going to call you Polly' – stirrings of embarrassment. 'You've put it better than any of us could' – meaning himself, people realized. In the same vein he continued for two or three minutes, so annoyingly that many wondered whether the friendly feelings for each other Mrs Langridge had encouraged needed to apply to everyone. Thus, many felt more confused and anxious when they shuffled into the April dusk than when they had arrived.

CHAPTER TWO

SO TO BED

AHEAD went Lorna Furnival. The first person she saw in front of her in the dusk was the Revd Charles Sage. 'Charlie', as he tried to think of himself and wished he could ask people to call him, but whenever he came close to suggesting it the words wouldn't come out. He'd just propped his bicycle against the gatepost and she saw him take off his bicycle clips, then come towards her at a shambling trot.

'Am I late?'

'You'll be late for your own funeral,' Lorna told him, a phrase of her mother's, though why it should come to her now, forgotten for sixty years, she couldn't imagine.

'Weren't we told nine?'

'I fear *not*.'

The Revd Charles Sage was their vicar, as far as they had one. 'Our roving Rev,' Chairman Fred Fisher would call him, since he served this and three more satellite parishes. Architecturally theirs was the most interesting church. The plan in the guide, for sale by the font but often stolen by tourists, showed that at least fifteen per cent of its structure was Norman, and coloured this purple, omitting to say that it was invisible because encased in Victorian stonework. But their church was probably the least attended, the Revd Sage's monthly Matins, followed by Holy Communion to save cycling, attracting only a tiny congregation, and his recent attempt at Evensong no one. Charles Sage, youthful, unmarried, faced the diminishing of his flock with a cheeriness which was less artificial than it seemed, since he enjoyed his heroic stand in an unpopular cause, though at the same time feared he was indulging spiritual pride. It was only occasionally, on winter evenings when he had no meeting or sickbed to attend and sat alone over a lightly boiled egg – he had digestive problems – that he needed to block terrifying doubts about the existence of the Supernatural. More often he was able to keep these away by being continually busy, hence regularly late. Now he stood still, unable to decide whether to turn back, or push past all these others advancing towards him. While he hesitated, a small wind came sighing up the valley, rustling the winter's dead leaves where they'd piled themselves against the hall's steps and stirring his girlishly fair hair, leaving a lock dangling over one ear.

'What a pity,' he murmured.

Lorna strode past him. Like Admiral Hawker and his wife, she carried a walking stick, though chiefly for attacking weeds or bashing soft drink cans into the ditch. As she reached the road she decapitated an early stinging nettle. She was less angry with Charles Sage than with herself for sometimes being a member of his flock. Sitting there, half frozen winter or summer, she would feel a mixture of contempt and sympathy for him, and the same for herself with less sympathy. Contemptible that, after Harry's death,

29

she no longer had the courage to stay at home, and she shook with annoyance, something she could normally prevent, so why not tonight? That assembly, of course. So many well-meaning fools. Well meaning? she asked herself.

Ahead of others, she was aware of a sudden quietness, the quietness she and Harry had noticed when they first visited the village, telling them they'd found what they were looking for. True she now heard the faint hoot of a steam train in the valley, but that was nostalgic, too; with an effort she could imagine it was a real train, bringing people home with shopping baskets, not a tourist trap. She could also hear to the west the relentless hum of motorway traffic; waking in the small hours it would sometimes take her a moment to realize what was missing. But her increasing deafness in her left ear to some extent protected her from this intrusion. Less easily ignored were those airport howls of jet engines ten miles to the north, though tonight, for once, they were silent. Far down in the valley she heard an owl.

Past the church she strode. Too early for swifts, each summer they still came to circle the steeple with endless squealing, just like the squealing of the children in the school playground, Harry would say. There had been a plan to block their nesting access because the bell-ringers objected to treading among their droppings. The Church Commissioners' architect had claimed that in another hundred years the accumulated dung would cause structural damage. Fiddlesticks! Harry had soon put an end to that. Difficult to believe that he'd been dead twenty years. More terrifying to think of the time they would both be dead even if, as she sometimes thought, seventy-three years were quite long enough to spend in one's own company, she sometimes told herself. And there were still moments when she was unable to believe that this could really be the end, to accept that it had never existed except for herself. It was this difficulty in believing in their own extinction, she supposed, which gave people what they called faith.

Just that one breath of wind and now such stillness that, fifty yards behind her, she heard someone speak. Not their words but a definite remark, then silence, as if he was listening, whoever he was, to see if he'd been heard. Less a remark than a shout. She peered back into the dusk but could see nothing. Close now to her garden gate, she used her stick to knock open the latch, looked above the silhouette of her house and had another surprise. There in the sky the moon had unexpectedly appeared above a monumental cloud which it seemed to sit upon, lighting its edges silver. Lorna Furnival slammed the gate and strode up her garden path. Horlicks with a nip of brandy was what she needed.

It was Mrs Volga (Vera Smithson) that Lorna Furnival had heard shout. She'd shouted at Mr Taylor, another absentee from the assembly, whom she could dimly see in the dusk in his garden above the road. He was still gardening.

'What do you do there?' Mrs Volga had shouted. It was the question many would have liked to ask. There was no answer.

She advanced to his hedge and peered. From here Mr Taylor's garden rose steeply, levelled, then rose again.

'Why are you digging all day long?' She spoke less loudly – this was why Lorna had heard only her first shout. It was another question many would have liked to ask, but only Mrs Volga had the boldness. Mr Taylor, at the top of his first terrace, seemed to be facing away from her. 'You have nothing else to do?' Often he was to be seen out here before dawn as well as after dark.

'I think it is beautiful.' In the dusk she could, in fact, see

31

only the shapes of a few shrubs. 'Soon it will not be here.' Her knowledge of the exact route of the County Road Plan was imprecise.

Though Mr Taylor, like his plants, was barely visible, it seemed to Mrs Volga that, instead of prodding the earth with some tool, he was suddenly upright. She was pleased. She had made something happen. She turned and swayed away. It was now that the moon came out, making her look (to Mr Taylor, who had turned his head, but nothing else) as dumpy as one of Snow White's dwarfs.

Mr Taylor was a new arrival in the village: he'd come a mere seven years ago. Wifeless and childless, he seemed perhaps 45, but behaved as if retired. Few could say why he disturbed them, and this was why they found him disturbing. One end of his garden was overlooked by the room which Gertie Jones rented from Ralph Gamble, in part payment for the weeding she did for him. Gertie Jones would describe to others Mr Taylor's gardening habits. 'He'll be planting himself before long.' It was she who'd first called him the Secret Gardener. As she set out each dawn to give Tobias his oats, she'd sometimes bellow at him, 'Hallo, Mr Taylor,' and he would seem to hear her with a shock of surprise.

'Lovely day.' Occasionally this was true, but she would also shout it through sheets of rain. Sometimes she hoped this would provoke him into a faint smile, but it was difficult to be sure with so much spray on her glasses.

Gertie was not sleeping in her room tonight, but had already reached Geoff Riddle's barn, where she intended to wedge herself among hay bales, as she usually did when she needed to rise early on eventing days. Tonight she was there for another reason: she wanted to be near Tobias, in case he needed her.

'There's nothing makes him nervous like knowing I'm nervous,' she explained to Geoff Riddle.

'Ah,' Geoff said, and then, after he'd worked it out, 'But suppose you wasn't here, how come he knows you'd be nervous?'

'He'd know,' Gertie Jones said. Some people were so stupid!

Beyond the partition she could hear Tobias snuffling and snorting in Geoff's dusty hay, and occasionally stamping, or, more correctly, disentangling his hoofs. Sometimes she thought she could hear his ears twitch, certainly hear the silence when both of them were listening. If any fucking road builder dare harm Tobias . . . Her heart pounded and she perspired into the camouflaged jacket, in which she planned to sleep.

'We found him in one of them old churns,' Geoff said, telling her the story of the escaped weaner. 'Just sitting there head first, he was. I reckon he thought so long as he only shows his arse we won't know where he is. All we needed to do was tip it up and pop the lid on.' He paused dramatically.

Gertie heard him pause but had no idea what he'd been talking about. She was imagining Tobias led away by some cruel stranger.

'Yes?' she asked, encouragingly.

'Only we couldn't find one.' Geoff Riddle paused for her to laugh. 'So Pike hunts for one while I sit on it. Lucky I come out whole, as they say.'

'So what'll become of the farm?' It was a question Gertie might not have thought it worth asking Geoff by daylight, but in the dusk she found she could forget his squiffy eyes and generally loony appearance.

The silence lasted so long she wondered if he'd heard.

'Bastards!' Geoff said.

'Enjoy the meeting?'

No answer. Geoff Riddle was imagining himself driving his tractor at them as they fled, tripped and fell face down in the mud.

At about the same time, Irma Svenson, whose home town was Malmo, was relaxing in one of Ralph Gamble's leather armchairs, both legs over one of its arms, in his sitting-room. 'You no want to fuck me?' she asked him.

Ralph Gamble winced.

'You think you have heart attack? How jolly.'

Ralph Gamble poured himself a gin, added a dash of angostura and stood with his back to her, staring out through the mullioned window of his mock Tudor stately home. His father had erected it after demolishing its thatched predecessor, when he'd arrived from Australia, rich from cleverly selling at the top of the sheep market, and set about building his way into the English gentry. As a little boy, Ralph remembered bricklayers at work up ladders so tall they seemed to reach the sky. He'd been given a child-size hod and marched about with it on his shoulder, carry-ing a single brick.

'So you are upside down.'

'Upset,' Ralph suggested. Yes, he was. Petty, it might be, but he couldn't help feeling that he hadn't been properly thanked for the Range Rover he had lately bought her. The problem was that if he hinted at this she would again laugh at him as she had at breakfast. Beyond her, through the window, the garden was almost dark, but he could just see the medlar tree which he used to run round, chased by nanny Bishop. He'd been born, his mother would tell him, in what she called the west turret, a grotesque outcrop above the billiards room.

'Ralphie,' he heard her say, in a tone which he recognized as an offer of peace. If only she didn't spoil things by being so crude. For a moment he'd even thought he might give her her marching orders. But he knew that he had only to turn his head and see her to forgive her. The truth was that his good luck still astonished him. Suppose that other gun had *not* brought his Swedish *au pair* as a beater. Remembering his first sight of her, knee deep in brambles, wearing that pretty hunting cap with a tall feather in it, still gave him a lift, as he liked to describe his need to adjust his trousers. So small and frail, so exactly what he realized he'd always been imagining. Not since Middleton minor at Sanderson's School for Boys . . .

'Lived here all my life . . .' he told her, still determined not to forgive her ingratitude too easily. 'Ouch.' She'd arrived behind him and given him a friendly clout on the backside.

'You old foggy.'

'Fogey,' he shouted.

They sat at the gate-leg table with the gin bottle between them. 'Urgh,' she said, and made a disgusted face each time she took a gulp. Presently she sat on his lap, though precariously because by then she'd begun to loll about. When they arrived upstairs and tumbled on to the four poster it turned out that lolling about was also all that Ralph Gamble could manage.

An hour later he eased himself out of bed to relieve himself, a tiresomely frequent need these days, then, more awake, weave downstairs to the gun room. There they all were, safely locked in their glass-fronted case – he'd dreamed that one was missing. He unlocked the cupboard's door and took down the 16, given him by his father on his sixteenth birthday. It might not have the killing power of a 12-bore, but the choke gave it at least the range. Once he'd brought down a red leg at seventy yards – his father had paced it out, up to his thighs in wet kale. He opened the breech, peered down the barrel, and remembered how, before modern powder, a gun needed cleaning whenever it had been fired. He snapped it shut, the sound telling him what a fine gun it was, half snap, half metallic clunk, not unlike an explosion in itself. He wiped the gun's metal with an oily rag where he'd touched it – sweat was acid – replaced it among its companions and swayed upstairs. She slept so peacefully. The moon lit only the bed's foot and beyond in the shadow he thought for an instant that her eyes were open and she was watching him, but her breathing was too even. He longed to wake her. Perhaps at dawn, though there had been failures then as well.

Though Ernest Boon knew that he should turn right when he reached the road and go home to his wife, Tiffany, to bring her a report of the assembly which she'd refused to attend, he instead turned left. He was opposite the church when he, too, heard the screech owl. Familiar these days as it was, its lonely call still made him shudder. But his attention was more on the tapping sounds ahead of him made by Lorna Furnival's walking stick. Perhaps now was the time to hurry forward and tell her. Easier in the dark when he couldn't see how she received it. Too late, a metallic clank told him she was opening her garden gate.

He'd had plenty of other chances. Perhaps he failed because he was afraid she'd laugh, tell him his interesting information was the sort of rubbishy rumour she'd been hearing for years. On the other hand he knew it was no rumour. He'd been in the department when a keen young clerk had discovered that one Harold Furnival had had what was then described as his hand in the till. His company's till. Legal action had seemed highly probable. True, subsequent investigation had suggested there wasn't enough evidence for a charge, but by that time Harry Furnival, who must have known his danger, was no longer with them. So his accident had perhaps been no accident.

It might anyway be best to hint, he thought, as he turned back towards the Hall, something he'd often concluded after a failure, leave it to chance whether or not she guessed what he knew. And if he ever told her, what would it lead to? A kind of intimacy in which he could admit his one-time love? More likely her cruel laughter. Long before he reached Meadowsweet, his half-timbered cottage, he was glad that he'd again decided to say nothing, so leaving himself with a sense of power, however uncertain, whenever he met Lorna Furnival. Like an orgasm, its fulfilment could lead to emptiness.

Up his garden path – herringbone brick, bordered with cushions of aubretia – Ernest went, veered past the front door's brass carriage lamp and arrived at the door of his kitchen. Through its glass panel he could see Tiffany's shelves of cork-stoppered food jars, above her shelf of spices in alphabetical order. In front of these stood Tiffany, swat raised above her shoulder, about to squash an early house fly on the breakfast bar.

'Well?'

Ernest Boon told her about the assembly and what had been decided – or, he admitted, not decided.

Tiffany snorted, struck, but missed. 'Bother.'

Ernest had been planning to end his report with something to make her laugh, but now thought it might be more amusing to grab one of his own feet and hop about on the other. He did this so convincingly that for a second Tiffany believed she might accidentally have swatted him. As a

THOMAS HINDE

result he was able to hop close and give her a calming kiss on the cheek. Far from calming her, his hopping told her that he'd been pretending, and as revenge she began to swat him. The swat was long and bendy, ending in a square of wire gauze, which hurt when she hit him about the head. Covering his ears with his hands, he went down on his knees. It was an age since they'd played this game.

Presently he sat back on to his heels. 'Like me to continue?'

'Please yourself.'

'He said we should form a committee.'

She considered attacking him again, but instead made another scornful noise in her nose, part laugh part snort.

'He'll be forming committees when we're dead and buried.' She meant the chairman 'I presume *she* was there.'

'Virginia?'

'Don't tell me there's another.'

'Not that I know.'

'Nothing would surprise me,' Tiffany said. 'You still think it's real?' She referred to Virginia Ranch's golden helmet, a problem they often discussed.

'Must admit I'm beginning to doubt it.'

Once they'd bet on it, but had lately begun to argue about which of them favoured hair and which a wig.

'Do you think she takes it off?'

'You mean when they. . . ?' But Tiffany was unable to make herself use the word and instead turned her back and began to bang the saucepans about which he hoped held his supper.

'Disgusting,' Ernest heard her say. 'She's only got what she deserves.'

Ernest was puzzled 'Got what?'

'Guess,' Tiffany said.

38

But Ernest wasn't able to. He suspected she wouldn't tell him because he'd caught her out, transforming something she still only planned to do.

Two hundred yards away, Admiral and Lady Hawker were passing the school when she dimly saw something white on the road and used her stick to spear it. Damp and droopy – there had been rain a few days before – it rose on her ferule, at first suggesting litter, then something more interesting. She detached it and peered. Too dark to be sure, but it looked like a letter.

Admiral Jack Hawker, failing to notice she'd stopped, was now several yards ahead of her, while their daughter, Briony, previously a long way behind her mother, had closed the gap. As a result they were now advancing in what Admiral Hawker would have called 'line ahead'. He was thinking of tench. What wonderful creatures they were. He'd once seen a four-pounder dug from one of Geoff Riddle's bone-dry ponds and put by Geoff into a cattle trough where the creature had given a couple of twitches of its tail then swum away as if nothing had happened. Briony, working hard with her short strong legs, was thinking of Sandra. 'Oh my darling,' she thought. She longed to discover Sandra in tears, after her chap had beaten her perhaps, so she could comfort her, and be given a tearful look of gratitude and love. Lady Hawker was thinking of the damp piece of paper she'd carefully pocketed.

In the kitchen she spread it on the Aga's yellow enamel hood. It was typed, she saw:

Dear Mr Fisher
We much look forward to your visit at 11 a.m. on Friday 1
May when our Chief Planning Officer will be pleased to
explain to you in more detail the implications with regard to

your parish of the recent amendments to the County Road Plan. In accordance with Government policy . . .

The rest was too muddy to read, but the district council's address was plain at the top.

Nothing wrong with that; it was Fred Fisher's duty to discover the facts. But the longer she stared at the grubby sheet the more it seemed to smell of dirty work. Why had he not mentioned it at the meeting? Anne Hawker reread the letter and made a plan. She'd dry it overnight then confront Master Fisher with it. 'Did you drop something?' she'd ask, and watch him squirm.

The three of them had been too preoccupied with their own thoughts to do more than glance at the one lit window of the school as they passed it. Inside, Miss Mary Wiggum sat at her desk, correcting Form I's efforts at the week's project – subject, 'The Life Story of the Common Newt.' In fact she had dozed and now woke with a jolt to face the deplorable scrawls and smudges of Justin Prone's effort. Below in the pile she would presumably reach that of Karen Prone, but not of Winston Prone nor of Howard Prone, both being still in Form 2. She had yet to meet their smaller siblings, Cheryl, Julie and Leonora Prone. *The neute is a ninsect*, she read, and there it was, quite a striking, long black thing, with an ambiguous but thickly outlined orifice at one end. 'Little monster,' Miss Wiggum thought, about Justin, not his newt, but, since no one was watching, allowed her wrinkled grey face to soften into a smile.

On the high ridge above the village, Mrs Shirley Prone bolted the door of 2 Keats Villas and stood in her dank front passage, listening. She could hear the telly in the back room, but who was watching it? that was the question. The kids, of course, but Billy might be with them. Slumped in one of her armchairs, no doubt, the great bulge of his belly show-ing between T-shirt and trousers. Six months ago she'd needed to escape from the tattooed arms of Billy Snipe and lock herself in the garden shed. Pity she'd been wearing no clothes and it was November, but she wasn't having another of *his*. She'd been a bloody idiot not to get her key back from him and the council wouldn't pay for a new lock.

Sounds of small arms fire then squealing car tyres from the back room. Shirley Prone lit up, took a deep suck, thrust out her breasts, not so fine as they were once, since those seven brats had been at them, and strode in. Just the kids, well, five of them, their eyes fixed on the screen, so they barely glanced at her. Wham, explosion, sheets of orange flame. Ignoring these she looked here and there about the room, still half expecting to find Billy in the shadows, grin-ning at her. A minute before she felt safe to land herself on the sofa, thrusting Justin and Karen apart with her bottom – 'Get over, you' – and attend to the corpse, its face smeared with plum jam, which the cop was prodding. At the same time she would have admitted, if given to admissions, that she was sorry not to have found some visitor, invited or not, waiting for her. She'd have liked to tell someone how she'd spent the meeting sneering at those toffee-nosed gits. Them and their stupid village. A new road might wake them up.

At the other end of the village street Joan Wodge, sent by her husband, Wilf, who couldn't leave his bar, and Evan Mullins, one-time shopkeeper, were near the point at which their ways parted: left to the Red Lion, right to the closed shop. So far they had accompanied each other in silence.

'Would you believe it!' Evan Mullins now said, express-ing his general view of life. It was all part of the same pattern that *he* should have been left to waddle home at one mile an hour with this half-size human being.

41

'Wasn't he lovely,' Joan Wodge said.

Mullins was speechless. Down there in the darkness she was almost certainly giving him a mad grin. Who could she be talking about? Not the chairman, the Lord preserve him from the possibility that anyone, even Joan Wodge, could describe Fred Fisher as lovely.

So it was the need for the company of someone sane that made him change his mind and turn with Joan towards the Red Lion.

Not another customer, and his friend Wilf glanced over his shoulder only for a second to make sure of this before returning to adjusting the amounts his inverted spirits bottles dispensed. 'Usual?' he presently said, as if putting the question to the bottles. Another full minute before he approached the bar and pumped two halves of bitter.

'Where you been this year?'

That was better. Anything other than aggression would have made Evan Mullins uneasy.

'Like to hear what I been through?'

Wilf held his beer mug to the light to stare through it, his message, 'look what the bastards are missing', and sucked at the froth.'Who do they think they are?' Mullins asked, starting with the chairman, moving on to 'her ladyship' the admiral's wife, then to 'the squire', in a mocking BBC accent, meaning Ralf Gamble.

Wilf Wodge didn't comment. One thing he did know about his profession was that he should never gossip about customers, even to a friend like Evan.

'That one should be done away with.' This referred to Bob Brandish. 'You know what he makes down there?' Evan Mullins described the Roman devices for laming horses, illustrating it on the bar with spilt beer.

Wilf was impressed. 'You reckon they'd work?'

'Don't ask me. It's the intent that's criminal.'

They thought about it in silence.

'Wouldn't you say?' Evan asked.

Wilf wouldn't say.

'Excuse me.' A customer had arrived.

Sandra was not down at the bottom of Lorna Furnival's wood being whipped by Bob Brandish, as Briony Hawker had fantasized. The two of them were lingering in the dusk not far from the village hall, waiting for everyone else to go home. They didn't exactly believe that their cohabitation in Lorna's caravan was secret, but instinctively behaved cautiously in case some council snoop should be spying on them to collect evidence for depriving them of the state allowances on which they lived, have their caravan declared unfit for human habitation, or discover they'd left Foxglove without a babysitter.

Bob *was* in a mood, Sandra could tell. He stood at the roadside, facing away from her, kicking something, she couldn't see. When he was like this it was better to say nothing. Reminding him she was near could turn his boot in her direction instead of what he was now kicking.

Bob was kicking nothing particular. But he was angry all right. 'What shits!' As bad as his father, worse in a way. At least he had the honesty to be a consistent reactionary. That lot! Pretending they wanted action then jeering at his suggestion. Those clever devices had pleased him ever since he'd seen one in a museum case of Roman artefacts. So simple, just four spikes correctly spaced and one had to land vertical. He'd show them. He gave Truffle's lead a vicious tug, bent to remove his muzzle and kick him in the hope there was someone still near enough for the dog to bite them.

'You sure. . . ?' Sandra began. Truffle had already savaged

43

the village's visiting fishmonger.

'Are you sure,' Bob mimicked her, and, noticing the village hall was still lit up, went for a stroll in the bushes which surrounded it. Annoyingly these were too prickly and the windows too high for him to get a good view and he could only see the chairman go past dragging something behind him. Bob approved of Fred Fisher. He was the sort of phoney the rest of them deserved.

The moon had gone behind a cloud by the time they set out, not taking the short steep path across Lorna's lawn, down through her wood, nor the path which led across meadows from Chestnut Lane, but a third, longer path which started from a point just short of Ralph Gamble's mansion. Sandra led, Truffle loped alongside her, Bob slouched behind. 'The village elders,' he thought bitterly. 'Elders' was the word. In a way they reminded him of all those layabouts the commune used to attract. Yatter, yatter, yatter, every day a fresh sponger would arrive, long on principles, short on action. That was where he and Sandra had met, and she had seemed different. Only later he discovered her silences weren't wise, but because she'd nothing intelligent to say.

Presently they were passing the six-foot iron railings which protected the 1930s' villa where Joseph Cuff lived with his white-haired mother. Joe Cuff was in the food business; some said he owned a chain of take-aways, others a pizza factory. He was a short, dark man of remarkable hairiness. 'Mr Woolly Bear', Gertie Jones called him, 'Esau was a hairy man', Fred Fisher had been heard to quote.

All was dark in the Cuffs' residence as the two of them sidled along the far side of the road. It was too dark for them to notice Cuff himself standing just inside his iron gate. Joseph Cuff had come out there to cool off. 'Just taking

Gideon for his walk, Mumsie,' he'd told her, referring to his
Alsatian. Whenever he went out or came home he had to
tell her – what a row there'd be if she needed him and he
was missing. Mumsie! When he imagined others hearing
him use that word he shook with rage. Sometimes it seemed
that his mother was laughing at the way she'd trapped him
in a childhood he could never escape.

He'd been out there only a couple of minutes when he
heard them coming, guessed they were the village dope-
heads. He'd teach them. Softly he opened the gate and
kicked Gideon out. Within seconds the two dogs were
howling and squealing as they gnashed at each other, rolled
each other over and tried to get their teeth into bits of hairy
flesh they could tear off.

'Stop them,' Sandra screamed.

'Can't you control your fucking animal?' Bob shouted at
Cuff, whom he now saw standing inside his open gate,
doing nothing to intervene. At that moment the moon re-
emerged from the clouds, making the silver ring in Bob's
nose glitter.

'This little piggy went to market,' Joseph Cuff shouted.

The dogfight ended as suddenly as it had begun, Sandra
dragging Bob down the pathway, Truffle limping behind,
snarling over his shoulder to save his honour. Cuff's insult
seemed to hang in the air and several times Sandra had to
drag Bob on, afraid that if he found a weapon he'd go back
and try to kill him.

'She's all right,' Sandra said, peering into Foxglove's cot,
trying not to show how relieved she was.

'Told you so.'

Late that night Bob left her making mint tea on their
paraffin stove, let himself out of the caravan, replaced the
log which kept its door shut and climbed again to the

village street, at one point missing his way and stepping ankle deep into the boggy surround of the largest of Lorna's ponds, on his way to the village phone box. He'd found a number for Mick. Mick would know where Perce was. They were the ones he needed for action.

Inside the village hall, as soon as everyone else had gone, Fred Fisher and Virginia Ranch had carried the coffee mugs into the kitchen to wash them, something they usually did after meetings. Often it led to other things. For example, Fred would grab Virginia from behind by the collar of her dress and tickle the back of her neck with his sharp black beard, at the same time using his free hand to take a handful of one of her buttocks – surprisingly ample because at a glance she seemed slim – and she would squeal in mock alarm. Then they would unroll the mat which the council had given the village some years ago for the promotion of self-defence courses in isolated communities. The mat was not much softer than the floor, but where they usually dragged it behind the hall's stacking chairs, was well hidden and less prickly than Gullies Wood.

Tonight it was as if the meeting had made their need more than usually urgent; Virginia had read in *Readers' Digest* that in times of plague people often began to behave lecherously. As Fred bumped up and down on her, trying not to come too soon, she let out an unexpected shriek. Fred was confused. Was it because of his fine performance which that moment had reached its climax? Or had he done her some internal injury? Adding to his distraction, her foot had struck the leg of a nearby whist table on which there were still some empty mugs. It swayed and recovered, though not before shedding a couple which shattered on the lino floor. Fred Fisher withdrew, shrank and sat up.

'What was that about?'

'Someone . . . I saw.'

'Who? Where?' She seemed genuinely shocked.

'Explain,' Fred said, with cautious annoyance, which would allow him to proceed to tenderness or move on to anger.

'The window . . . a face.'

'Don't believe it.'

'I'm sure . . .' But now she seemed to be trying to convince herself. There was a long pause as they stared at each other and listened. They always reduced the light to a single fluorescent tube on these occasions and in the low light she seemed to grow more rather than less astonished by what she'd seen. 'Eyes,' she said, and began to fasten her bra and drag on her panties.

Fred pulled on his trousers and went out to scour the bushes, as he would have described it, though in fact he gave them a sharp glance, and decided they were too prickly. Dangerous, too. Suppose he barged boldly among them and suddenly felt hands around his neck?

'Nothing to report,' he told Virginia.

'You are brave.'

'Oh, I don't know,' Fred Fisher said, pleased, but not entirely certain she wasn't laughing at him. With Virginia Ranch he was never quite sure.

At the top of Chestnut Lane where he and Virginia both lived they separated, believing as usual that no one had seen them together, and set off, Fred first then Virginia a minute later, for their respective homes. Ahead she saw a crack of light appear briefly then disappear as Fred opened and shut his front door. Now she reached her own doorstep, felt for her key and trod on something slimy. As she bent to investigate, a repulsive smell rose to meet her. Virginia Ranch screamed.

47

She used her pocket torch to make sure. About six inches long and a horrible yellow colour. And squelchy, so that there was some on the side of her shoe as well as more that she could only smell clinging to its sole. She fetched a shovel from the garden shed and set about scraping and wiping. All the time tears ran down her cheeks; she couldn't stop them. Who would do such a thing?

Luckily she hadn't opened the front door so perhaps Michael hadn't heard her scream. More luckily, as soon as she stood in the front passage she heard the telly in the sitting-room. Safer, nevertheless, not to go straight in there but let him hear her in the kitchen. Presently, as she loaded the dishwasher she knew he was behind her.

'How did that go?'

'I don't know. Quite well, I suppose.' She realized that she'd forgotten whether she was loading or unloading. Behind her, Michael was staring down at her. Why did he have to be so tall, she thought. She knew that she had not been thorough enough and Michael had smelt it.

Fifty yards further down the lane, 'How was that?' Wendy Fisher asked her husband, Fred. He stood behind her, watching her kneeling beside the sofa, changing Jamie's nappy.

'Spiffing,' Fred said.

'Meaning?'

'Brilliant.'

Wendy, who had a teaching diploma, disliked the way he misused that once useful word, but extricating the truth from what he told her was always a guessing game.

'I think I stirred them up, got them to agree . . .'

A performance. But tonight she was too tired to listen, yanked at the nappy's adhesive strip, heaved Jamie on to her shoulder and made for the door.

'So to bed,' Fred Fisher called cheerily.

CHAPTER THREE

NOW YOU SEE IT

THE days following the assembly were anxious ones, especially for Fred Fisher. At an annoyingly early hour next morning he was visited by Lady Anne Hawker.

'This yours by any chance?' She held out the letter she'd found in the road the previous night, Aga-dried but mud-stained.

'Let's have a squint.'

While Fred Fisher stood at his front door examining it, two small children arrived from behind him to peer round his trouser legs, distracting and annoying Anne Hawker.

'So what are you up to?'

'What me!' Fred Fisher said, implying how absurd it was to suggest that he might be up to anything, though at the same time grinning in case the old bird should find this difficult to believe.

'Yes, you,' Lady Hawker said. As well as being married to an admiral she was the daughter of another, a more distinguished one, in her opinion, whose height she had inherited so that, at six foot two, she looked down on Fred Fisher, five foot six. Now one of the children put its head between his legs at knee level and stuck out its tongue, though only for an instant before it disappeared, dragged from behind, no doubt by Mrs Fisher.

'Sorry about that,' Fred Fisher said, trying with one hand to bat the other child out of sight. 'If you'd like to come in I'm sure I can explain . . .'

Disconcerting as he found it that Lady Hawker seemed not to hear this invitation but stayed staring down at him on his doorstep where, instead of using her walking stick as a suppport she was gripping it near the top like a weapon, he had for a moment been more alarmed that she might have found one of several other letters which would have needed careful explaining. As a self-employed financial consultant – adviser on stocks, bonds, pensions, insurance, mortgages – he had several clients whose properties might be much enhanced in value by the proposed motorway, and a couple of these had written to him suggesting that his position as chairman of the parish council which opposed the development gave him a conflict of interest. Still more worrying, he had received subsequent letters thanking him for promising to take account of their interests. Fortunately the letter she'd found was harmless. It was important that he should maintain friendly contact with influential members of the district council.

'A powerful lobby may support us,' he explained to the tiresome lady. 'Many of them doubt the merits, even the legality of the County Road Plan. By no means impossible that the council will back a further appeal . . .'

Comforting as it was to hear himself justifying himself in this way, he was all the time trying to remember whether he had taken those other letters to the Assembly and perhaps accidentally scattered some on his way home. To his relief she presently, if rather rudely, turned her back on him and strode away. 'Golly, what powerful legs,' he thought, as he watched her retreat, but only when she reached the lane and he was sure wouldn't turn back, retired to his study.

Here he knelt beside his desk and began to hunt through the pile of papers he'd taken with him. Still no sign of what he was looking for when he heard his study door open and knew that his wife was behind him, staring down at him but saying nothing, as if her surprise at finding him down here on his knees was silencing her.

'Oh hallo,' he said, sitting back on his haunches. 'Can I help?'

Several more seconds before she seemed to recover. 'It won't spin,' she said.

'The washing-machine? Oh dear. Shall I come?'

But she'd gone. Since he had a poor record as a home plumber this was probably for the best, he reckoned, as he rose from his knees, sat at his desk and from habit switched on his PC. A touch or two on the mouse and it offered him a blank screen. Had he unconsciously hidden those letters where he didn't need to see them, he wondered, and discovered that, in a tiny font he'd typed 'Help.'

As if in answer help arrived, in the form of a plan. Silly of him not to think of it before. The new committee he'd promised them, would not be a suspect subcommittee of the parish council, but have a separate identity. And it could have a different chairman. 'No longer responsible', he already imagined himself reassuring those clients. The more he considered this solution the better he liked it.

The first hint of a further problem came the following morning when Virginia Ranch failed to arrive for their weekly meeting to discuss parish council matters.

'I hope she isn't ill.'

'Not exactly,' her husband Michael Ranch said. 'More shocked, I think.' Standing at his front door, his long pale fingers hanging by his side kept stirring as if they had a life of their own. 'Wouldn't you be? Put yourself in her position. Finding it there in the dark.'

'Oh.'

'Well, almost dark. She could have trodden in it.'

Gradually Fred guessed the truth.

'Did you examine the evidence?'

'Scraped it away, as much as I could.'

'Like me to give you a hand?'

That afternoon the two of them spent half an hour poking and prodding among the immaculate alyssum which lined the path to the Ranch front door. 'There's this,' Fred Fisher said, spiking a yellow sausage-shaped fragment, but before he could hold it up for inspection it crumbled. On the doorstep there was a yellow smear, but that told them nothing.

'I could call the police.'

'I wouldn't do that,' Fred Fisher said, in alarm.

'She cries all night.'

Fred was impressed.

'Who would do such a thing?'

Fred could have made a suggestion. He tried to remember whether Tiffany Boon had been at the assembly.

Next day the first of several expensive bunches of flowers was delivered to the Ranch residence, inconspicuously, Fred Fisher hoped.

Doctor Sweet also visited the Ranches. He was a neat, grey-haired man with small pale hands but virtually no short-term memory, regularly forgetting what he last prescribed for his patients and often to which of them he was speaking. Some in the village who still believed that medicine was a variety of magic complained at such waywardness. Some had other complaints. 'The cheek of it!' Mrs Shirley Prone said, when he'd advised her to tell her current lover, Billy Snipe, to use a condom.

'The damned thing had disappeared,' Admiral Jack Hawker would say when he told the tale, as he often did, of Dr Sweet emerging from a call to give advice about his lumbago, and finding he had no car. After a moment the two of them had seen it freewheeling downhill 100 yards away where it finally drifted into a hedge.

'You know what he gave that one?' Polly Langridge would say, about the occasion when her husband, Sam, had missed his step and fallen up to his neck into the sewage soak-away in the valley which it was once his duty to inspect. 'Aspirin!' But Polly wasn't angry. Though it confirmed her distrust of doctors, it was a good laugh.

Certainly Dr Sweet's visit to Virginia Ranch produced no immediate result.

'They do say 'tis chronic,' Polly Langridge told Sam as she scraped fragments of toast, soggy with baked-bean tomato sauce, into the cat's bowl. The mysterious disappearance of Virginia Ranch interested her increasingly as it grew longer. Lying back on the sofa, legs stretched forward, Sam wriggled his toes. He was giving these an airing, so making his splayed feet seem even more curious since each big toe ended in a bulbous swelling the size and colour of a ripe plum. When asked how he had once been the village's fast bowler, Polly would say these were 'what give him his push.'

'That's what they say,' Polly continued, referring to the mystery of Virginia Ranch.

Sam belched.

But none of these developments prevented a feeling

spreading in the village that they had all become over excited at that assembly, tricked into alarm by Fred Fisher. Nothing had happened yet and perhaps never would.

Briony, the Hawkers' daughter, was the first to discover otherwise, when, early on the morning of the day scheduled for the meeting which would create the new committee, she set out for the walk she often took across the meadows which lay on the far side of the stream that bordered Lorna Furnival's wood. From here she could look across the stream to the shabby caravan which Bob Brandish and Sandra shared. Once she'd been lucky enough to see Sandra squatting outside its sagging door, scraping clean a wok. The sight of those pretty little hands busy at this menial task had caused Briony's chest to heave with fondness.

Not a sign of either of them this morning, though their evil grey dog was chained as usual to a nearby tree where it watched her in a way that suggested how it would savage her if let loose. Less usual, she also saw, about ten yards further from the caravan, a thin stake about three foot tall with a piece of red cloth attached to its top. To warn people not to trespass on their herb garden, Briony guessed, but then saw a similar stake about twenty yards to the right of the first – then another, then another . . . They seemed to form a line. Briony was puzzled, a state of mind which made her cross. When she saw a similar line of stakes running in the same direction some fifteen yards above the first line among the trees of Lorna's wood she grew more puzzled and cross – till suddenly she understood. The horrible motorway, of course.

She also understood what she must do. Across the shaky bridge she went and, starting from the first she'd seen near the caravan, began to stumble from one to the next, jerking them from the ground and tucking them under her arm.

Loaded with as many as she could manage, she recrossed the bridge and began to hurry across the meadow, because she knew she was stealing. It was when she tried to carry them over the style into the next meadow that some became entangled with her legs. Losing her balance, she tilted forward, felt several snap under her great weight while others were jabbing her in rude places and finally landed with a thud on the far side, turning her ankle. How odd the foot looked, at right angles to the ankle, she thought, and for a moment wanted to laugh, then the pain arrived, more than she'd ever thought possible, making her whimper then howl. Not since she'd fallen off Smudge aged ten. 'Oh oh oh,' she sobbed.

It took her an hour to climb out of the valley and reach home, where she told her parents she'd slipped on an empty 7UP can. And where, after another half-hour, they'd wrapped her in a powder-blue bath robe and her foot in a massive bandage, and sat her in front of a fire.

Sandra had been invisible to Briony because she was inside the caravan, making nettle soup. They were at their best in May, bursting with folic acid, fantastically good for the immune system – she could tell from the way, even when cooked, they made her stomach tingle. And they were *her* veg, seeing she was Taurus. In fact, she was Aquarius, if her stupid mum hadn't made a typical cock up of the dates, but Taurus was what she preferred. From the soup she would occasionally turn to look at Jemmy, a small duckling which lay in a feathery but shitty nest at the foot of her daughter Foxglove's cot where she, the duckling, occasionally opened its beak to give a faint quack, this sending Sandra into a new paroxysm of pity. The other four ducklings had been found as little mangled corpses lying around the coop where Aspidistra, a genuine Rhodie borrowed from Geoff Riddle, had hatched them. She and Aspidistra had almost given up hope, not knowing that duck eggs take twenty-eight days. Sandra had accused Bob's wonder dog, Truffle, of the massacre. 'Fox,' Bob had said.

Presently, still some hours before Briony was to arrive, Bob had woken, lit a hand-rolled fag not much thicker than a matchstick and squeezed past Sandra to go out for a piss. That done, he'd taken Truffle to help him water the hemp seedlings he'd planted behind Lorna's glass house with the hose which brought their drinking water from Lorna's scullery. If the dog nibbled a few so what? Showed he knew what was good for him. Each time he touched Truffle's unhealed wound made by Gideon's teeth, now more than a week ago, the poor dog snarled with pain. Trust a capitalist fucker like Joseph Cuff to have an Alsatian to protect him. Well Mr Cuff was going to learn what happened to persons who couldn't control their dogs. Plenty of ways to extinguish the brute, Bob was thinking, when, glancing back past the caravan, he saw the nearest of the stakes with its red tag. He, like Briony, then saw others and guessed their purpose.

He returned to the caravan to consult Mick and Perce but found them still snoring on the floor of what Sandra called the caravan's fo'c'sle. Prodded with a foot, they only groaned. Ah well, Bob thought, it would give him time to decide how best to present his plan to them.

This he did when at last they woke, but still sat on the floor, sipping mugs of mint tea. It wasn't original, he admitted, but so what? What was wrong with borrowing an idea which had proved it worked? Near Honiton a single protester had been dug in so deep he'd held up the fucking contractors for weeks. Now was their chance because he'd discovered the exact route the motorway would take. Bob led them out to show them. 'While you two lazy sods were still snoring . . .' he began.

For the next ten minutes, while Bob searched among the trees for marks in the earth to prove he hadn't been dreaming, they followed him, dancing around him, jeering at him and suggesting he have a brain scan.

Bob let them have their fun. But he didn't give up. Later that day, when he had found several places where the earth had probably been disturbed by those stakes, the three of them stood together among the trees discussing where best to start digging. Perhaps he'd inherited from his father the dislike of being defeated, which had helped the poor sod to climb the ladder of local government.

'So who's going to be the lucky miner?' Mick asked.

'Don't we have a leader?' Perce said.

Bob, testing the earth with a spade, let the silence grow. 'I might,' he said, over his shoulder. The truth was that this had been his plan from the start. When the *Gazette* ran the story, along with his own name, there would be his father's. 'Son of County Council Chairman, Sir William Brandish, leads village protest.' That would teach him. True, his father had ways of bullying editors into leaving out his name, but he'd deal with that problem if it arose.

Meanwhile, since they couldn't survive for ever on mint tea and wild garlic, and the village shop's rubbish would one day be exhausted, he'd thought of an alternative. Up through the wood he went, past Lorna's house, across the village street, up the rise beyond so as to approach Mr Turner from above. No sign of him at first, so he found a place where the surprisingly high barbed-wire fence was lowest and was astride it when the weirdo came out of his garden shed rushing towards him, fork in hand.

'Who are you? What do you think you're doing?'

'Couldn't make you hear from below,' Bob lied.

The man stopped a couple of yards away, where he stood, holding his fork at hip level, as if it was a rifle and bayonet.

Now that the shop had closed, Bob explained, they had nowhere to go for vegetables. Did Mr Taylor by any chance have any to spare? They'd pay of course. Perhaps it was because he was having to remain uncomfortably astride the barbed-wire fence that he seemed to be failing to explain calmingly. He and Sandra were gardeners themselves, he began again, hiding a laugh at their solitary patch of hemp. They'd like to get to know another keen gardener, he said, and risked lifting his second leg to get it across the barbed wire and clear of his testicles – but instantly stopped as the man jumped closer, both feet at once.

Looking past him, Bob saw a large dumpy person wearing the sort of felt hat boys once wore for cricket, arrive in the doorway of his garden shed. Ah yes, Mrs Volga. As she came closer, Bob repeated to her his enthusiasm for gardening in general and particularly the sort of garden which all village cottages once had.

'But it is not cottage garden,' Mrs Volga said.

'Oh yes? May I see?'

Under her protection, as it were, Bob was shown the big trench, the two-dozen seed boxes at its bottom with their unhappy-looking seedlings, the garden shed – but this only from the outside where he read a notice, KEEP OUT. In its doorway, Mrs Volga blocked his entrance, while Mr Taylor stood nearby, fork still at hip level. Both seemed to wait for him to leave.

'So about vegetables . . .' Bob began.

'He is not growing things to eat.'

'Oh well.' Glancing past her as he turned to leave, Bob saw other notices on the shed's inside walls. EXTINCT ILLEGLE.

At the front gate, where she followed him, she told him,

'He is not being dangerous, only frightening of you.'

'You're telling me,' Bob called back, from across the village street.

At about the same time that morning Polly Langridge was making her discovery. 'That give me quite a turn,' she told Sam, back in their cottage.

'The buggers,' Sam said.

'I suppose it ain't right to blame them personal like,' Polly said, but without conviction since she hadn't actually seen whoever had brought it.

Sam thought about it. 'Where did you reckon it was?' Suppose he put nothing too heavy in his bucket he might go past it on his way to his daily swabbing of the village toilets, provided the going wasn't too rough.

'There ain't no reckoning about it,' Polly said.

So they set off together, down the lane which led to Ralph Gamble's mock Tudor mansion, but reaching first the tall iron railings of Joseph Cuff's 1950s' villa. Here Polly stopped, and stood looking down the path which led alongside the railings down into the valley.

'So?' Sam said.

'You telling me it weren't here?' Polly said. ' 'Cos it were, 'cos I seed it.'

'And it ain't now.'

'Bright yellow it were, with a great big arm thing.'

'Didn't you say bulldozer?'

'What if I did?'

Polly set off down the steep path, looking for wheel marks, but the ground was too dry and there were anyway lots of old criss-crossing ones. Occasionally she looked back at Sam, but didn't expect him to come down because of his feet.

'What was you doing anyways, nosing about here?'

59

'Mushrooms,' Polly said.

'Mushrooms in May!' Sam gave a harsh laugh and started back towards the village to top up his bucket and do his swabbing.

So it was only Polly who heard two gunshots from the direction of Mr Gamble's place. 'For that matter, what's *he* doing,' she asked herself, 'killing little birds when they should be still in their little nests?'

It was Irma's doing, bless her, Ralph Gamble admitted.

'Why are you looking so down of the mouth?' she'd asked him, between spoonfuls of muesli.

'*In* the mouth,' Ralph corrected her. 'I didn't know I was.'

'Am I looking down in my mouth?'

'Certainly not.' That was true. She was looking as bright eyed as – the only animal which came to mind was a ferret.

Even so he wasn't prepared for the moment when, after draining her coffee cup, she sat herself on his father's tiger rug and started, one after another, in a purposeful but at the same time absent-minded way, to take off her socks, jumper, bra, jeans, in fact the lot except her panties.

Afterwards they'd fallen asleep together under a blanket which she'd thoughtfully provided and it was not till an hour later that he'd dressed and gone out with his gun to check his latest hatching. Poor little bastards, he thought, with unusual understanding of their life expectancy. It was partly to warn them of their fate, as well as to celebrate the event of the morning (a relief after the disappointment of the night of the assembly,) that he'd fired both barrels at the sky, and watched them scatter in panic.

Polly climbed back to the lane and set off for the village. Though cross that Sam wouldn't believe her, she quickly recovered and, from the banks she passed, picked a bunch of primroses in case they came in handy. The morning was turning lovely, the sun lighting the new leaves of oaks a soft brown and of beeches a bright green. Ashes were still bare, she noticed. 'If the oak before the ash . . .' she recited. Now a horse came trotting behind her. Must be that Gertie Jones, what's always cheery, though she can't see no further than her nose without them great glasses.

Gertie had been telling Geoff Riddle, stabler of Tobias, of her latest observations out of the window of the room she rented from Ralph Gamble in the village street. She was now grooming Tobias in Geoff's stable yard.

'That was the big hunt, last night,' she said, speaking to the one of Geoff Riddle's eyes which stared at her as opposed to the one watching the donkey, Moses, twenty yards to his left. 'Out there till past one in the morning, no kidding, with a thing like a searchlight.' She was talking about the Secret Gardener.

'Slugs?' Geoff Riddle suggested. 'You never know.'

'*You* may not,' Gertie Jones told him. 'What's he dug that great trench for?'

'There's plenty you can put in a trench.'

Gertie Jones was unwilling to quarrel, because of Geoff Riddle's modest charge for Tobias's livery. 'Get over, you,' she shouted at Tobias, kneeing him affectionately in the belly.

'There's spuds.'

'Just now he's had a visitor,' Gertie continued. 'Two, to be exact. And then there's a great shouting match with that Mrs Volga.'

Gertie squelched across an area of cow dung as big as half a tennis court to fetch Tobias's saddle. Behind her she could hear Geoff Riddle warming to his subject. 'There's mulch. There's bones' – this on a higher pitch. 'Anyhow, slugs doesn't need a trench. When you squash 'em they're nothing but slime.' Successfully he switched eyes without turning his head and stared at her with his left while his right considered his line of derelict machines. Gertie rode off, soon passing Polly Langridge, on her way to the Ridge, nearest place for a canter.

Polly didn't hurry but stopped here and there to give news and receive it, so that anyone listening from a distance might have heard her begin, 'Waarl, they do say . . .' but not what they said because Polly would confide this in a stage whisper, watching for the impression it made.

'Waarl they do say they slips him a bit,' she confided to Lorna Furnival whom she'd found sitting on a stool in the churchyard, dabbing with a brush at the canvas in front of her.

'Oh that is lovely, oh I does admire that,' Polly continued, about Lorna's foreground of daffodils.

'Who slipped what to whom?' Lorna asked.

'That would be telling,' Polly said coyly.

'And why don't you?'

'Oh I do so *love 'em*,' Polly said, reverting to the daffodils. 'Wish I could do painting like that.'

'I expect you could if you tried.'

Lorna knew that she couldn't paint, but she also knew – had known ever since she was widowed – that she was not going to spend the rest of her life running the Women's Institute. The problem had been, and still was, to decide how she *would* spend it.

'Are you saying someone's been bribed?' she asked.

'Oh, I wouldn't know about that.'

'I'd have thought you do know, or you wouldn't have mentioned it.'

'There's some as puts two and two together.'

All her life, secrets had made Lorna cross though she

tried not to show it.

'I reckon it's a right shame,' Polly said.

Lorna tried staring at her. What an old bundle. But annoyingly she was now looking up at the church steeple and pretended not to hear.

'Must be getting along,' Polly said.

'I should hope so,' Lorna Furnival told her canvas.

Fifty yards up the street Polly had spied Mrs Volga and now set off in that direction. They met opposite Mr Taylor's garden.

'I like to ask you question,' Mrs Volga began.

'Up to you,' Polly said.

'Each day I see you walk this way, that way. What is it you do?'

'Well I like that!' Polly thought indignantly, turned away and called up to Mr Taylor, whose back was turned as he dug, 'What be you a-burying there?'

Even if Mr Taylor had answered she would not have heard him, because at this moment, her eyes rising to the ridge above the village, she saw it. Silhouetted against the blue sky, it was in full sunlight and, just as she'd said, was a brilliant yellow.

'Didn't I tell that one?' Polly said, referring to her disbelieving husband.

Though it was far away up there, Polly could tell that it was huge. Or was it? The curious thing was that when she thought about it later she couldn't decide just how huge. Sometimes she remembered it as small and distant, sometimes vast and looming. Later, when Sandra returned from seeing it (nominally collecting wild herbs for Foxglove's tonic) she, too, discovered that it was pulsating in her memory, now retreating into the distance, now advancing, till it seemed suspended above the village.

'There it be,' Polly said, determined to make the most of her triumph. 'Didn't I say?' Beside her, Mrs Volga began, 'In my country . . .' but got no further. Nor did others seem sure what to call it. 'That's plant,' Sam Langridge said, returning, bucket in hand, from his work. 'That's a digger' someone else said. Others gave it initials and Polly would later sometimes call it 'that GBD' or sometimes 'that there GDB thing', but after being put right several times favoured, 'That G blithering what'sitsname.'

Perhaps it also frightened Tobias, when he arrived from the lower ground beyond the ridge. One moment there Gertie Jones was trotting him towards it, the next he was disappearing the way he'd come, hind legs rising as high as Gertie's riding helmet as he tried to unseat her.

Meanwhile, a cluster of Shirley Prone's children had arrived fifty yards along the ridge at the end of Keats Villas, where they stood staring at it as if wondering what useful pieces they could detach from it.

Curious too, some noticed, that it didn't seem to have a driver. Whoever had brought it had apparently abandoned it. Nor had anyone heard its engine, though this didn't prevent them hearing in their heads the grinding, clanking roar it might soon be making. Its lack of any human controller somehow increased its horror – hardly too strong a word – which gave some the sort of sinking shock that the certainty of death gives at four in the morning.

All day people passing up and down the street paused to look up at it. Gertie Jones brought Tobias, behaving himself properly again, to show it to him from a safe distance and prove it wasn't dangerous, only for him to shy violently when he saw mop-headed Bob Brandish, back among the upper trees of Lorna's wood to spy on what was happening. About midday a Range Rover approached; Irma Svenson's gift from Ralf Gamble. He'd sent her when rumours reached him, to discover what was happening. Dwarfed by its size, wearing enormous black sunglasses, she had to hoot loudly to get past these peasants; she was the third cousin of a Swedish baron. Distracted by this, she forgot to look up at the ridge at the right moment and never saw it.

That afternoon the sky, which had been so bright and blue, became overcast. Clouds, grey with silver edges, swirled and heaved, as if busy up there about their own affairs. Soon after dinner, Sam Langridge discovered that the leaves of his tomatoes, prematurely planted out, had turned a nasty grey.

Though there were various places from which it could be glimpsed between the cottages which lined the village street, there was no better viewing point than where Polly Langridge had first seen it, over Mr Taylor's hedge and up his steeply sloping garden. As the afternoon passed, those who kept gathering here became aware of Mr Taylor's increasing agitation. He came and went more often from his porch to his garden shed, then back to his porch, for no clear reason, now carrying a fork or a seed tray in one direction, then carrying it back.

Soon after four o'clock, by which time quite a crowd stood along Mr Taylor's hedge, he suddenly came rushing down the slope towards them, violently shaking something in front of him which rattled. When he began to run up and down his hedge, thrusting this towards them in turn, they realized that it was meant to be a collecting box, improvised from an empty baked-beans tin.

A moment later he dropped it, ran back up the slope and returned carrying a hoe in a threatening manner. One who had arrived at the hedge was Admiral Hawker, who now believed he was being attacked and raised his walking stick as if to engage Mr Taylor in mediaeval combat. Some later said that stick and hoe became entangled, but if so only for a second before Admiral Hawker, without his support, lost his balance and sat heavily on to his backside.

'Fornication', he cried.

Confusion followed, and by the time Admiral Hawker had limped away, his arms over the shoulders of one-time nurse Tiffany Boon and Billy Snipe, Shirley Prone's current lover, Mr Taylor had disappeared.

'Well, who would have thought it!' Polly Langridge asked those left behind.

As six o'clock approached the numbers further diminished since this was the time for the new defence committee to hold its first meeting. Those Fred Fisher had invited assembled at the new vicarage, a prefab bungalow erected by the Church Commissioners on wasteland near the graveyard, quite adequate for an incumbent who showed reassuring signs of remaining single, so enabling them to sell its five-bedroom Victorian predecessor and profit by the exchange.

'Good of you to submit yourselves,' the Revd Charles Sage welcomed them, faintly grinning as if hoping others might find this verb mildly amusing: they didn't. Ten of the eleven Fred Fisher had chosen came, only Admiral Hawker remaining at home, where he sat resting his bruised coccyx across the fireplace from his daughter with her bound ankle. Mrs Volga,uninvited, had also arrived, bringing with her Mr Taylor, surprisingly, considering what had happened so recently.

Fred first explained at length the reasons for forming a new village defence committee. 'Assuming most of you have noticed today's development,' he ended, 'I don't need to convince you that matters are urgent. Officially there is nothing more any committee can do. The government has spoken and we must submit. That's what it thinks. Our business is to show it, politely, but if necessary, impolitely, that it must think again.' Encouraged by his own oratory, he ended, 'New blood is what we need.' Laughter from Lorna Furnival. 'So what I suggest is that we first elect a new chairman. Any volunteers? Don't all shout at once.'

No one shouted and a long discussion followed, since many wondered how they could elect someone without any candidates. Mr Taylor asked, 'Why?'

'You mean?' Fred Fisher prompted him.

'I mean why?' he repeated, so fiercely that it suggested he might be missing some garden tool.

'There's some as has more than enough to do as t'is,' Polly Langridge suggested, since she didn't consider whatever Fred Fisher did to be real work.

'Where's our Member, that's what I'd like to know?' Ralf Gamble asked, referring to their Conservative Member of Parliament who had failed to promise to defend pheasant shooting in his last circular.

Lady Hawker spoke privately to Lorna Furnival, explaining that she had come alone because she had two invalids at home, suggesting a picture of those two large persons bundled up opposite each other which made Lorna chuckle.

Beside Fred Fisher was an empty chair. There Virginia Ranch should have sat, but she remained absent. Annoyingly, because Fred had hoped that offering her as an efficient secretary would encourage a new volunteer for chairman. Her husband, Michael Ranch, who brought her apologies and offered to take her place, was no substitute.

Ernest Boon said nothing, too occupied with watching Mr Ranch while pretending not to. Like almost everyone else he'd heard of Virginia's disappearance. 'Don't suppose *she'll* be on show,' his wife, Tiffany had said.

'Why's that?' Ernest had asked.

'How should I know?' Tiffany had said.

Did she know? Ernest wondered. After thirty-seven years he still found it difficult to know if she was lying. Their only son had not had this difficulty, he remembered, but Graham had chosen to escape to the most distant habitable place on the globe where he'd married a Maori.

At other moments Ernest glanced at Lorna Furnival, then quickly away. In company the temptation to hint to her that he knew something interesting about her husband's supposedly fatal accident seemed unthinkable. But if he ever met her alone would he perhaps be tempted?

Joseph Cuff, who had arrived ten minutes late with a roar of his BMW and crunching of gravel, also said nothing, but listened with what Lorna Furnival once called his 'fixed snarl'.

Miss Mary Wiggum said she was sure some of the more sensible boys in Class 1 would be glad to help.

Allowing time for all this and more – essential, Fred Fisher had long ago discovered, for managing meetings – he eventually told them he detected a consensus that there should be a secret vote, everyone naming the candidate of their choice: not true but a way to force them to make up their minds with which he'd come prepared. When no one protested, Michael Ranch distributed slips of paper, collected them, counted them and declared the result. One vote for Lady Hawker, eleven votes for Mr Fisher.

'Well, well,' Fred Fisher said. 'I don't know what to say.' This was true, but only for a moment. 'I should have explained,' he began – and then, in a way he later found it hard to understand, heard himself saying things he'd never intended to say. Partly he was genuinely flattered by the vote confirming his popularity and their need of him. Partly, from the moment he'd thought of his plan he'd had to surpress a reluctance to surrender his power to influence events, not to mention many opportunities for public speaking, which his chairmanship gave him. But what at this moment tipped him into doing the opposite of what he'd planned was a sudden realization that he would one day have to tell Virginia what he'd done and the way she would be disappointed, even contemptuous. 'However, if this is your genuine wish,' Fred Fisher said, 'I shall reluctantly bow . . .'

Too late he began to suspect that there were other explanations for what he'd done. Why, he asked himself, had *he* voted for Lady Hawker except in revenge for the way she'd scared him ten days ago? Serve her right, he'd thought. Let *her* do better. So why had those eleven chosen *him*? Also perhaps as revenge. He'd got them into their present mess: let him get them out of it.

Soon after dawn next day, the clouds gone, and another hot one by the look of it, Geoff Riddle, inspecting his hay meadows, noticed something red at the foot of the style between the ten-acre and the glebe.

'What silly bugger. . . ?' he muttered, stumped along the hedge and discovered a bundle of stakes each with a red tag. Angrily he gathered them into a bundle and carried them to the stream where, one after another, he flung them across it towards a thick clump of bushes.

At the centre of these, Ernest Boon crouched, holding his binoculars and listening to the dawn chorus, so wonderful in these early weeks of summer. One after another sticks with red tails began to fall around him. After the first couple he drew his jacket over his head and held it there with both hands. 'Quite like Agincourt,' he thought, and wondered if this might be the best way, dramatic and somehow manly, to report this humiliating episode to Tiffany.

That day and for several more the great yellow machine remained on the ridge above the village. On the third day the Prone children, skirmishing more boldly from Keats Villas along the ridge, began to clamber over it, chipping at its paint with sharp stones, tugging at bits of metal which might come in handy. On the fourth, Justine Prone stuffed clay up its exhaust pipe and was disappointed next morning to find that it had got away without exploding.

'Orders countermanded,' Fred Fisher had told anyone who asked him for an explanation, hinting that he might be responsible for this apparant retreat, but would rather not reveal the tactics he'd used.

CHAPTER FOUR

A MARCH

MISS Wiggum marshalled them in front of the school. They had four banners, made of old sheets on which Class 1 had written slogans in drippy, red paint: SAY NO TO PLAN, WE ARE A VILLAGE. Mary Wiggum was particularly moved by GO AWAY YEW, the contribution of Hilary Stitch, the nicest but not the brightest of her girls. The wind was a problem. Though it was now the first day of June, the sky was full of racing clouds, and small arms struggled to hold up poles provided by Geoff Riddle, as gusts filled and flapped the sheets. There were twenty-nine children. Missing was Winston Prone, but Justin Prone had brought a message for Miss Wiggum.

' 'E catched it. Me bruvver.'

'Try saying "brother", Justin. It's not difficult. Caught what?'

Justin crossed his arms over his stomach, bent sharply forward and made a retching noise.

'I understand, Justin. Now stand up straight.'

'I catched it first, miss.'

'Yes, Justin.'

'Then me sister Cheryl.'

'I dare say, Justin. Now please get in line.'

'Then me mum,' – with a sideways lear at a friend. 'Oo, it was 'orrible.'

'Justin, that's quite enough.'

'Well, I thought you oughter know. Me mum says we got it from that thing.'

'What thing?'

'What we climbed on.'

'That's quite impossible.'

'Me mum says anything's possible.'

'Ridiculous.' But because she didn't like to be so snubbing Miss Wiggum added, 'I forgot to tell you I liked your drawing, Justin. Of the newt.'

'That's all right, miss.'

What an odd boy, she thought. He talks to me as if it's I who need comforting.

At last the column set off towards the church, Miss Wiggum leading, helpful Mrs Stitch, Hilary's mum, shepherding behind. They should sing, she thought, but what? 'Onward Christian Soldiers' didn't seem right. Soon they reached Lorna Furnival's house where they made a fairly orderly about turn. As they returned past the church Miss Wiggum knew what it should be. 'And did those feet,' she began, at a rather gruff pitch, 'in ancient times . . .' She'd got no further when she felt her skirt tugged from behind.

'Yes, what is it?'

She didn't need to be told. There at the foot of the churchyard wall lay young Howard Prone. His legs had apparently collapsed under him. His eyes were shut.

Annoying as this was, it was hardly surprising. In such a slovenly home, germs were bound to spread. More disturbing for Miss Wiggum was her discovery, as she struggled up from kneeling beside the fallen boy, that another small circle of children had formed behind her. At its centre was Elsie Patch, lying flat on her back, her eyes wide open, as if staring at the sky but not seeing it.

The march threatened to disintegrate. Banners swooped and an excited mixture of jabber and squeals spread. 'Silence,' Miss Wiggum called. Fortunately at this moment Tiffany Boon, ex-nurse, appeared and went from one casualty to the other taking their pulses.

'Both alive,' she shouted.

'On we go,' Miss Wiggum called, leaving Tiffany now joined by her husband, Ernest, his tufts of owl-like hair erect with concern, in charge of the casualties, and the march began to straggle forward.

Moments later, Miss Wiggum noticed a curious figure at the roadside with pointed hat and small pointed black beard, which had let half the procession pass but was now dodging towards her.

'So you decided . . .' he began.

'What's that?' she shouted, the wind making it almost impossible to hear, now sure that this gnome-like person was Mr Fisher.

'If I remember rightly . . .' Fred Fisher tried.

What he remembered was that, at the new committee's first meeting, a march had been suggested. 'Splendid,' he remembered saying, then, because he favoured private negotiation at which he could better hide his conflicting interests, had persuaded them to appoint a March Subcommittee. And that was the last he'd heard.

'As a school governor . . .' he tried again.

'Governor be blowed,' Miss Wiggum shouted, astonishing herself. Though she was trying to keep calm the wind and the events so far had stirred her up. 'Excuse me,' and she escaped to help three of her girls whose banner had been blown horizontal.

As the procession progressed, several people opened their windows to stare and some waved, then shut them again because of the wind. At the roadside, Gertie Jones and Briony Hawker, still propped on a crutch, stood together watching. Their unlikely friendship had begun when Gertie, exercising Tobias in that same meadow, had yelled a greeting to Briony, lurking half hidden in its hedge.

'If you keep leaping around like a kangaroo he'll land me in the ditch,' Gertie had yelled, and Briony had emerged, pretending she hadn't been hiding, and apologized to Tobias. She had been a rider herself till her weight made suitable mounts a problem. 'She's a proper sport,' Gertie now told Briony.

'Who?'

'Miss Whackham.' Though Gertie Jones never looked for human company, Briony was a change from all those 'horsy arseholes' of the neighbourhood most of whom Gertie had quarrelled with.

Now they reached the garden of Mr Taylor, the Secret Gardener. Pinks, candytuft, flowering currant, yellow broom, huge banks of scarlet cistus – the garden was nearing its summer climax. That strange trench at the centre had gone – or had it? Searching for it, Miss Wiggum was astonished to see Mr Taylor's upper half appear among a line of wallflowers, apparently kneeling in it. Was the poor man so shy he was trying to hide there, she wondered. A gust of wind bent the wallflowers, hiding Mr Taylor, but bringing their scent, most wonderful of the summer – mown grass apart – taking Mary Wiggum back to the Dorset cottage where she'd been a child, her mother's borders, the happiness all flowers but especially scented ones still gave her. Next year she must make Class 1 plant some – if there was still a school next year.

Suddenly the children in the rear heard a high-pitched squealing of tyres and, looking round, saw a bright red car hurtling towards them. It came so fast that it swerved violently, right then left, before stopping slewed across the road, only a couple of yards from Hilary Stitch and her banner.

Almost at once it began to move again, though at a walking pace, and a short hairy arm appeared from its side window, followed by a moon face which began to shout. Many were relieved, sure that they were being encouraged, but a moment later they heard a terrifying hooting and it came charging at them again. Panic followed as they ran right and left, only just escaping as it began to force a way through them. The face still shouted and now they could hear what it was saying: 'Who do you think you are? This is a public highway.' The hand was making a V sign.

That should teach her, Joseph Cuff thought, as he drove into the distance, tyres still squealing at bends, well pleased with himself. He was not thinking of Miss Wiggum whom he'd barely noticed and certainly didn't know by name, but of his 78-year-old mother, the only person he didn't dare bawl out. This morning she had been at her most ungrateful.

'Joseph, I don't eat bran,' she'd told him.
'But the doctor says—'
'Prunes,' she'd said fiercely.
'Mumsie, we've tried them.'
'No we haven't.'

Loss of short-term memory? Cuff thought. Not bloody likely . . .

Most, of course, knew Joseph Cuff, the pizza tycoon. From his villa just outside the village he would drive through it twice a day since this was his only access, often at 60 mph.

'You gotta be sorry for him,' Polly Langridge would say, and wait to be contradicted. 'Covered in all that hairy black stuff.' Unanswered, she would continue provocatively, 'What about his poor face then?' It was true that this was covered in dark freckles; some said there were more freckles than face.

It was now that the children, looking away from the disappearing car, saw Miss Wiggum sitting at the roadside, holding both hands to her face. Those who were close could tell from her heaving shoulders that she was sobbing. 'Wetted her knickers,' a friend told Justin Prone and was disappointed to get no approval for this amusing suggestion. Now several of the girls had also started to cry. 'It didn't oughter be allowed,' Justin said, and went to fetch one of the fallen banner poles which he broke into a handy length.

From a roadside bank which Fred Fisher had mounted in haste to escape that alarming car, he watched till it was hidden by a bend in the road. Lunatic, he thought, but that didn't drive away a disturbing idea, which he should have had long ago. Just because the new road would cross and destroy the field which lay behind Joseph Cuff's house he wasn't necessarily opposed to it. On the contrary, since he owned that field he might be planning to making himself just enough of a nuisance to earn whopping compensation.

Late that afternoon the rain came. For hours it fell heavily, creating streams along the sides of the village street, turning Ralph Gamble's pheasant chicks, who stupidly refused to shelter, into stork-like caricatures. Below Lorna Furnival's wood it filled her black ponds. Around midnight there was a sudden crash of thunder. It seemed to happen directly above the village and was so violent that some thought it must be a plane exploding. Many lay awake, waiting for what might happen next, but there was only silence. Even the rain seemed to have stopped.

Next morning the sun rose behind trees sparkling with rain drops, so charmingly it seemed they were pretending nothing had happened. Few were deceived. All who had seen or been told of the disastrous end to yesterday's march remained shocked.

'In my country at once the police are putting him in prison,' Mrs Volga told Fred Fisher, met at the school gates where he was delivering two young Fishers.

'And chopping off his head,' Fred Fisher said cheerily.

'Why are you such a funny man?' Mrs Volga asked.

'Born that way,' Fred Fisher said. 'Ask me another,' and escaped into the school playground.

Behind him he heard Mrs Volga say, 'But I ask and you do not answer,' while she let herself into Mr Taylor's garden. If the rain had flooded his trench, it could have ruined his life's secret work. It shouldn't be allowed, she thought, instinctively blaming the capitalist authorities, but with half her mind also blaming the storm itself, though they could well have arranged that as well.

In the school Miss Wiggum sat at her desk, also untypically angry. Surely there was a passage in the Bible beginning, 'And the wicked shall be punished'. She would have liked to read it at assembly, but her head was in such a fuzz because of the double dose of pills she'd needed before she could sleep that she couldn't find it. She was also worried by an extraordinary picture, of a sort she hadn't had since her own school days, which kept arriving in her head: a clay model of a small stout man stuck with pins. 'Behave yourself, Mary,' she told herself, but it kept floating back.

'That one oughter 'ave 'is 'ead examined,' Polly Langridge said. 'Who does he think we are? Le Monz or something?' She was speaking to Bob Brandish, met in the village street, advancing with long strides, his shaggy lurcher behind him. Quickly he changed direction to pretend he'd not been going the way he had been going, but too late. Polly Langridge had seen him hide something behind his back.

'What would you expect?' Bob said, looking at his shoes, jerking the dog's lead for no clear reason.

'What would *I* expect?' Polly Langridge asked, with mock astonishment. About to expand on this, she caught a smelly gust of wetland vegetation from Bob's combat jacket which nearly choked her. Though to be fair his shoulder-length, matted hair, with the sun filtering through it, almost looked clean.

'See you soon.'

As he strode past her it didn't escape Polly's notice that he was again going in his original direction. Nor that it was an envelope he was hiding behind his back. 'Ah,' she said.

Behind him Bob could hear her repeating this syllable in a variety of tones, suggesting the tuning of a musical instrument. He could still see her though a hedge now separated them. Above this her head showed, staring at him as if she believed, ostrich like, that she was fully hidden.

For a month Bob had been screwed up with anger every time he examined Truffle's wound. It had begun to fester. Much as he regretted it, he was Sir Rupert's son and had inherited an objection to being defeated. But he'd still done nothing. It was Sandra's description of the march that transformed his private anger into a cause. She had drawn the picture, when they'd managed to find a clean sheet of paper. Give her her due, she could draw well. He had written the threatening message – with his left hand of course.

Presently he reached those six-foot iron railings with spikes on top, slipped the envelope into the metal post box welded to their inside and hurried on. No red car in the drive, as he'd calculated, but suddenly a hideous barking as the Alsatian rushed out of a kennel to stand against the railings on its hind legs, teeth hideously bared. Bob gave it the finger and turned quickly down the footpath. Glancing back he saw the curtains of an upper window separate and between them a face, white hair . . . Stuff her.

Ten minutes later he reached the caravan and found, as he'd expected, those two big-mouths chatting with Sandra as they sipped mint tea.

It was them, not the tree roots who worried Bob. Mick, it turned out, suffered from claustrophobia. What would you expect from the great authority on mining? As for Perce, he was just a lazy bugger. While it was Bob who worked away at the face, more than twenty feet in now, mud in his hair, mud smearing his T-shirt and jeans. Because it was at the bottom of the hill the ground was wetter than he'd expected. As he scraped and dug he would faintly hear them at the mouth of the shaft, laughing. Several times he might have come up and yelled at them if crawling backwards didn't take so long.

Now he passed them without a word, dressed himself for the job, collected the cord and earth bag and began the descent. The sodden ground was a problem. Wet lumps kept falling off the roof. Much of the way he'd had to use wooden roof props. Deeper it might be drier. Or might not.

The bag full, he jerked the cord, faintly heard the bell and Truffle barking. No response. Typical. But, angry as they often made him, today he was comforted when he thought of 'the shock Mr fucking Cuff would get when he arrived home tonight'.

In these days many also continued to speculate about the strange sickness affecting the village children. Not strange to Admiral Jack Hawker, because of his experience of ceremonial parades. If one rating fainted, within a minute half-a-dozen others would have keeled over. On his back lawn, his bruised coccyx less tender, he would think of those long-ago ceremonial occasions, and consider the rumour of a plague to be female panic.

His wife was less sanguine. 'Three more gone down today,' she told him one morning.

'Gone what?'

'Down.'

'You don't say!' The admiral was unimpressed.

'I intend to call the doctor.'

Polly Langridge laughed when she heard of this. 'You know what that one'll give'm,' she told Sam. 'Castor oil – that's binding and no mistake.' In fact, Dr Sweet took the epidemic seriously. Diarrhoea was one thing; sudden loss of consciousness another. Absent-mindedly he prepared to take Howard Prone's temperature by the anal method, a throwback to his student days in Paris.

'What *you* up to then?' Mrs Prone asked, seeing his hands undoing the boy's belt, wondering if it was her lucky day and she was about to witness a genuine paedophile at work.

'Abdominal examination,' Dr Sweet explained.

Others were equally baffled, and presently – who started it no one could say – a sinister explanation spread. To force them to submit, the village water supply was being spiked.

'They gotter learn we wont be druv,' Polly Langridge said.

The only person to believe fully that they were being poisoned was Sandra, who turned off Lorna Furnival's hose and began to get drinking water from a patch of swampy ground near one of Lorna's ponds. If she dug a hole there, then waited till the mud settled it came more or less clear. That didn't matter much anyway because of the fantastic minerals mud contained. You could tell by how *real* it tasted. 'Foxglove agrees, don't you, darling.' Three days later, she and the baby were also vomiting. 'Stimulated my immune system,' she told Bob, between spasms. 'Getting rid of impurities.'

But others took the possibility of sabotage seriously. Ralph Gamble watched his young pheasants anxiously. Could it explain why they still hung around for corn, reluctant to take off? Too bad if they decided to let him down by dying before he could shoot them. Irma Svenson washed her blonde hair morning and evening with disinfectant shampoo.

Polly Langridge, meanwhile, reported her meeting with Bob Brandish to her husband. 'So who would *he* be writing to?' she asked. 'You old farter,' she added, when he wouldn't answer.

'There's dozens,' Sam said. He was having a baked beans snack at the kitchen table.

'And where's the post box, that's what I ask?'

'Hundreds, thousands,' Sam continued.

'But why should *he* be writing to them, tell me that?'

This momentarily defeated Sam. He suspected that Polly

was intentionally muddling him.

'I tell you what that one's a-doing,' Polly said.

Sam sulked.

'Luggin bits of wood around like that. He and his lot down there, what be they up to?'

Sam filled his mouth with beans. Poor old Polly. Been coming on for weeks.

As the days passed it began to seem to some that they were surrounded by things they did not understand. Others began again to wish that something definite would happen to prove they hadn't been needlessly stirred up.

They did not have to wait long. A week later, at around eleven at night, those who were awake heard the wailing of an approaching ambulance. It came at high speed down the village street and stopped outside Lorna Furnival's, where she and Sandra were standing. 'Cunts,' Sandra screamed. 'Fucking fucking cunts.' It had been twenty-five minutes before they'd arrived. Lorna, in her dressing-gown, held Sandra's hand, but she continued to sob hysterically.

Ten minutes later, the fire brigade arrived and after about half an hour managed to carry a suction pump down into the woods where they eventually managed to pump the hole sufficiently dry for a fireman to crawl down with a rope.

In the light of the searchlight which they'd fixed to a tree, Bob Brandish's appearance was distressing. He was wearing only a T-shirt and underpants. Because the tunnel was narrow, pulling him out by the rope tied round his chest and under his arms, had yanked his head sideways so that it seemed almost to be part of his shoulder. Occasionally something caught the light there: his silver nose ring.

Mick and Perce were nowhere to be found. Nor, later, was anyone able to remember where exactly the end of Lorna's hose had been found, or whether it had been pouring water.

CHAPTER FIVE

POST-MORTEM

THE village defence committee met in Fred Fisher's front room. Here there were green china frogs on the mantelpiece and polished incidental tables set with coloured family photos in silver frames. Areas behind the chintz-covered three-piece suite, on the other hand, were cluttered with Lego, whirling plastic toys and wooden railway lines. There was also a faint smell of urine, and from upstairs came occasional yells followed by unexplained silences.

Present were Lorna Furnival, Admiral Jack Hawker and Anne Hawker, all with their walking sticks, Ernest Boon with his wife Tiffany who had fought with herself but lost before coming to this house of immorality, Mrs Volga with Mr Fisher, Gertie Jones, taking time off from her jobbing gardening, her employer Ralph Gamble, surviving village farmer Geoff Riddle and failed-shopkeeper Evan Mullins.

Missing for reasons still not understood was Virginia Ranch. So was Briony Hawker for a reason more generally guessed but nevertheless surprising. Briony had replaced Bob Brandish in Lorna's caravan. Here she and Sandra had lain all night in each other's arms, Briony's enfolding Sandra while she sobbed. Together they had poked mushy peas down the gullet of Jemmy the duckling who was beginning to look as if she wanted to live, but disappointingly suggesting she might be a drake. Briony had reduced by six inches Sandra's shoulder-length, matted hair, Sandra had massaged Briony's ankle with oil of dandelion and they'd both made Foxglove giggle by cooing at her. Admiral Hawker had written to his solicitor asking what were the rights of a parent.

'I don't imagine I need say that recent events have been a shock,' Fred Fisher began.

'Don't say it then,' Lorna Furnival muttered.

'We can hardly afford to ignore what has happened.'

They had had no choice. A week had passed during which most had found it impossible to avoid speculating about the tragic event in Lorna's wood. They had asked each other many questions but got few satisfactory answers. Why was he down there on his own at that time of night even if he had quarrelled with his two friends? To prove something to them, or to himself? Why had no one bothered to see where the hose was? Why had those other two hippies run away and where were they now? Surely it must all mean something, but what?

Briony questioned Sandra, as gently as possible. When had she last seen Bob's two friends?

No answer.

'When you went out to look for him?'

'I don't know,' Sandra said. 'I really don't know.'

'Sleeping where they usually slept?'

A sniffling sound.

'You see, the police may question you so you should be prepared. It won't matter so long as you know where to find them.'

'But I don't.'

'Their names then.'

That did it. Briony took Sandra in her arms.

'I told him he shouldn't,' Sandra sobbed.

'Shouldn't what?'

More tears.

'Go digging a mine at night?'

Sandra nodded, but whether because an answer was being forced from her or because it was true, Briony couldn't be sure.

The morning after the accident, if an accident it had been, several policemen arrived, and trampled round the mouth of the hole, destroying any footprints there might have been, then attempted but failed to interview Sandra who screamed at them and bolted herself inside the caravan. It had only been later that afternoon that Briony came knocking at the caravan door, carrying a supermarket bag which held her toothbrush and tube of toothpaste. Meanwhile an enterprising young constable had discovered a bed of suspicious seedlings behind Lorna Furnival's glasshouse and taken one away for analysis.

Next day a reporter from the *Gazette* arrived, and Briony spoke to him through the caravan window. This was not easy because the window was small and low, with the result that she suggested to the young reporter Alice in Wonderland after she'd drunk from the enlarging bottle.

'Might I have a word with you, miss?' the reporter, Keith Haresnip, began.

Briony scowled at him.

'I don't want to intrude.'

'Who are you?'

The young man explained.

'I can't ask you in,' Briony told him.

'Oh, don't worry . . .'

'And I wouldn't if I could.'

'It was you, I believe, who raised the alarm.'

'It was not.'

'You are . . . I mean, you had been living . . .'

'I'm not who you think and anyway it's none of your business.'

'You and the late Mr Brandish—'

'Rubbish,' Briony said, and slammed the caravan window so violently that it sagged in its rotting frame, leaving only a two-inch gap at the top. 'Clear off,' she shouted through this.

The reporter was still encouraging himself with the editor's advice, 'Persistence, that's the key, young man,' when the caravan door opened and a terrifying hound bounded towards him, yelping as it came.

Back in the village street, his shins bleeding from bramble lacerations, the young reporter had the luck to meet Polly Langridge.

'I bin down there and took a look,' she told him.

'To the scene of the tragedy'

'There's things needs explaining, wouldn't you say?'

'I was going to ask you that.'

Polly stared at him but didn't answer.

'Things like. . . ?' he encouraged her.

'Imagine *you* bin down a hole.'

The young reporter preferred not to.

'And you finds a trickle coming your way.'

'Yes?'

To his dismay, Polly Langridge's face creased in agony; like others in the village she was now suffering from what her husband, Sam, called 'the runs'. Unaware of this, the young reporter thought her distorted face must be her answer and nodded sympathetically. 'I see what you mean.'

'I bet you doesn't.' Slowly she recovered from the spasm. 'Well what would you do? You'd come crawling out fast, wouldn't you? You wouldn't wait around to be drownded.'

'But suppose there was a dip in the shaft. Suppose this had filled before he realized and trapped him.'

Polly had also heard this suggestion, but it didn't interest her. 'And where's all that water coming from, you tell me that,' she said and hurried away. Though less affected than some, there were limits to what she could endure, and as soon as she reached Gullies Wood she found brambles thick enough to hide behind and relieved herself.

Continuing to forage along the village street, captions forming in his head – MYSTERY DEATH IN DOOMED VILLAGE – Keith Haresnip was surprised as he glanced up a sloping garden to see a tall clump of flowers – old fashioned phlox, though he didn't know it – shaking violently, while other plants all around were still. The longer he stared the more peculiar it seemed. Unaccustomed to the supernatural, he began to shudder when, close to the ground, a hand appeared.

'Hallo there,' he called, to reestablish normality.

Instantly those flowers stopped shivering and, sun-hat first, a man rose, as it were, from the earth.

'Bad year for weeds,' Haresnip ventured.

'*Terrible*,' the man said.

Haresnip had foreseen discussions of the weather, of the cost of living – it was a time of rapid inflation – of the reckless way people drove nowadays, leading naturally to the village's recent tragedy. Instead, he found himself continuing down the village street. The ghoulish way in which the man had used that single word was enough to prove that he'd found another product of in-breeding. 'Many thanks,' he called over his shoulder.

He'd gone only a few more paces when he heard a loud, unexplained rattling noise approaching him from behind. Quickly it grew louder, came closer and swept past. Someone on rollers. Not just any someone, but a girl. Not just any girl, but the most amazing girl ever. She wore black skating boots, black knee pads, black elbow pads and a black cyclist's crash helmet. Within these came very short shorts – and a tiny T-shirt, exposing the most wonderful nut brown skin he'd ever seen.

The young reporter, who was engaged to a local hair-stylist whom he found none too exciting – apart from her well-developed breasts – had a vision of what true love might be like. Words like 'awakening', 'apparition', 'bowled over' hurried through his mind.

Ten yards beyond him Irma Svenson, who was testing the new toy Ralph Gamble had given her, turned and came sweeping back, knees bent, those wonderfully tanned legs crossing and recrossing while she sped towards him. As she passed their eyes met and they exchanged a glance which the reporter interpreted as total understanding, not just of his own marital predicament, but of the cool detachment with which he viewed this. Now he found himself turned through 180 degrees and starting in pursuit. Too late, Irma was fifty yards away and soon all he could make out was that black helmet and those black pads strapped to her elbows. Soon even the rattle of wheels on tarmac faded.

Stuck at the road centre, he was now being approached by a woman in a formidable bundle of clothes. The day was bright, the morning sun already hot, but she seemed wrapped for the Arctic.

'You are missing?' she said.

'What, me. . . ?'

'Missing your way.'

'Well, yes, I suppose. . . .'

'Who are you? I do not know you. What do you do?' Mrs Volga watched him with the kind of warm intimacy which terrified him and was not unlike the early approaches of his fiancée. It was only because Mrs Volga's one-time husband, Mr Smithson, had found such generosity of spirit a delightful contrast to the inhibited English that they had stayed together for ten years, until one morning, not much different from any other, he had fled.

The reporter explained his business. 'Incidentally,' he added, 'who was that?'

But this lady seemed not to have seen what to Keith Haresnip was already acquiring the nature of an apparition. How could someone be so blind? Instead she was waddling away from him. 'I show you,' she called over her shoulder, but without turning her head, as if her clothes were making this difficult. Down Chestnut Lane they went and there found Fred Fisher in his front garden, oiling the wheel of an inverted pushchair. 'He is our leader,' she announced.

'Oh, I don't know about that,' Fred said.

'I'm Keith Haresnip,' Haresnip explained.

'Oh!' Fred Fisher said, in a tone which suggested he would do his best to believe it.

'From the *Gazette*.'

'Ah yes!'

'My friend here tells me you are the organizer of local resistance. With reference to the recent tragic event, might some people hold you responsible. . . ?'

'What an extraordinary suggestion.'

'You knew about the tunnelling?'

'I certainly did not.' This was untrue. Rumour of what had been happening down there in the woods had reached him via Polly Langridge.

'Would you say certain things need explaining?'

'Indeed?'

'Where, for instance, did the water come from?'

'It's been raining. Perhaps you hadn't noticed.'

'Are you suggesting the hose wasn't responsible?' The encounters of the morning, especially with this vast foreign lady who still hovered behind him, had sharpened his manner. Long ago, when he first chose his career he would imagine himself speaking in such a threatening way, an amalgam of TV investigators, but this little man with his sharp black beard was bringing it out.

'I know nothing about that.'

'I thought it might be the sort of thing—'

'You'd better think again.' Fred Fisher jerked the pushchair on to its wheels and pushed it backwards and forwards. No squeaks. Success.

'Should something occur to you . . .' Keith Haresnip turned away and started up Chestnut Lane.

'Remind me of the name of your editor,' Fred Fisher called after him.

Three days later the inquest took place, but was adjourned by the coroner until the cause of death was known.

Meanwhile the *Gazette*'s story had appeared under the headline HORRIFIC DEATH OF SHERIFF'S SON. Sir Prosper held this honorary position, but the editor instantly drew a line through it. 'Do you want our well-educated readers imagining it's some boring piece about Robin Hood?'

'I suppose not,' Haresnip said. 'If we added DOWN HOLE . . .'

Now the editor stared at him in a more threatening way, as if wondering whether he was being sent up. Haresnip's story had hinted at many of the case's suspicious features, but most of these had been subbed out or mangled. Though he was sorry the body was no longer described as 'lurid green', he was pleased that the village's chairman appeared as Mr Frederick Fishnet.

The funeral, when finally allowed by the coroner, had taken place on the afternoon before the meeting of the village defence committee. Sir Prosper Brandish, recognized to be sharp even by those who thought him pompous, had considered not attending, guessing that most of the congregation would think he was secretly relieved by the death of his embarrassing son, but was persuaded by Lady Brandish who was also intelligent but less pompous, though she also had mixed feelings about attending, understanding that her husband was responsible for her son's way of life – and death. Lorna Furnival had not meant to attend and didn't.

'Lord forgive them for they know not what they do,' the Revd Charles Sage began his address.

'Hear that?' Gertie Jones whispered loudly to the person on her right, then on her left. Both pretended not to hear. 'Who says he didn't know?'

'May I suggest you keep quiet,' a voice in the pew behind hissed. Gertie couldn't see who because her spectacles had steamed up.

'Suggest what you like.'

'Would you mind leaving?' someone across the aisle said.

'I'm going, don't you worry.' But in the church porch she could still be heard shouting and stamping. The truth, unknown till now and only now dimly realized by herself, was that Gertie Jones had fancied Bob Brandish. That silver ring dangling from the centre piece of his nose, had been quite a turn on – possibly because of its equine suggestions. Now they'd killed him. She wasn't certain who they were,

92

but knew someone had.

In a back pew near the door, sat Keith Haresnip.

'What makes you think you can squeeze any more out of that one?' his editor had asked, but fortunately was distracted by the phone, allowing Haresnip to slip away. Now he was making notes on a slip of paper hidden in the printed Order of Service leaflet.

Only when the service was over and the coffin being carried out was he rewarded. There she was, conventionally dressed, but, with hair revealed to be so blonde it was almost white, she was if possible more arousing. Round her neck she wore a gold chain and round her black dress a gold belt. As she passed, surely for an instant she caught his eye. If only she hadn't been holding the arm of that village ancient with jowls like a bloodhound's, old enough to be her dad.

So it was that next day Fred Fisher had plenty to say when he opened the committee meeting and proposed to outline 'the current state of play'. But the longer this took the more he sensed that he was being listened to with less than usual respect. Some were stirring in their chairs, and presently he could hear murmurs. Before he had said all he would have enjoyed saying, Tiffany Boon interrupted him.

'You seen this?' She held up the *Gazette*.

Most had, but none said so.

'They hit *you* off all right.'

No one else spoke, but their silence left little doubt that she had spoken for many.

'I'll be the first to admit that things are not all going our way,' Fred Fisher conceded, when, to his relief, there was another interruption.

'Come right in then,' he called to Polly Langridge, who had put her head round the door. 'Make yourself at home.'

A moment later she was followed by her husband, Sam.

'Any more for the ride?' Fred Fisher called.

'You just carry on, far as you got,' Polly told him, sitting heavily and fluffing out her cardigan – like a broody hen settling on her sitting, Geoff Riddle thought. Others noticed that Polly had brought a book which she now opened on her lap.

'Some of you,' Fred began again, 'may think that the cautious approach we have so far adopted has been mistaken. Nevertheless, recent events – I refer to the protest march – suggest that perhaps—'

'Shambles,' he heard Admiral Hawker say. Jack Hawker had been distressed by Bob's death, remembering the chats he used to have with the lad about carp and tench, not to mention that tin of damn good maggots.

'Why, look at this here,' Polly Langridge said, leaning across Ernest Boon to show Geoff Riddle. It was a book of historic photographs. 'Why, there be old Pa Snipe.' She put a finger on a straw-hatted labourer, erecting corn shocks in Geoff's top field. 'He bin a one and no mistake.'

'Are you suggesting. . . ?' Fred Fisher began, but no one was sure whether he was speaking to Polly or answering the admiral. The admiral, meanwhile, grew red in the face with anger. For 'suggestion' he had misheard 'digestion'. What damned rubbish – his stomach was one organ which had never let him down.

Fred Fisher now listed the useful meetings he'd attended, correspondence he'd had with people of influence and conversations with others who might be just as influential, though he regretted that their names were confidential. At one moment he was distracted by a noise he couldn't identify, though those sitting near Lorna Furnival knew it was jabbing the floor with her stick.

'Look at that now,' Polly Langridge continued, leaning in the opposite direction to show Ralph Gamble a sepia photo of the demolition of the old manor house by Ralph's father, in preparation for its present neo-Tudor replacement. 'That be your old dad.' She pointed to a tall moustached figure in ankle-length overcoat and top hat, watching the works.

'I suppose we might form a committee,' Ernest Boon interrupted with daring irony.

'Well, would you believe it?' Turning in her chair, Polly Langridge held up her book to Sam. She'd found a photo of the defunct village cricket team which included Sam himself, in white flannels but black boots. 'Well strike me!' As the years had passed she'd perhaps begun to doubt his reputation as one-time village fast bowler.

Further discussion followed as Fred continued to invite constructive ideas, but when no more came he told them not to despair because no date had yet been fixed for the Minister's final, irrevocable decision.

'And that will be the end of the matter,' Lorna suggested.

'I wouldn't be so sure,' Fred said. 'There's one piece of news which I hope you'll find encouraging. Our Member has given me a firm undertaking that before then, in fact in the very near future, he and the minister will visit us.'

He'd saved this trump card to the end but the response was disappointing. Looking from one to another of them he found none that would meet his eyes. Or rather only one and hers he couldn't properly see because of her grotesque glasses. Gertie Jones. So far Gertie had said nothing, but those near her had been increasingly aware of her heaving chest and were afraid that when she did she would be embarrassing. They were right. 'You know what?' she now said. 'We got traitors.'

Traitors? What did she mean? 'Could the lady explain?'

Admiral Hawker asked.

Gertie would not explain and in answer to more questions remained obstinately silent. It was only when Fred Fisher was declaring the meeting closed that she interrupted loudly, 'We better find out then, hadn't we?'

CHAPTER SIX

PLAY TIME

WHAT had Gertie meant, Fred Fisher wondered?

Yes, there was Mrs Stitch who came to clean – worrying, even though his study was supposed to be a no-go area. And Mrs Stitch almost certainly knew Polly Langridge because everybody did. Sitting at his desk, he might another day have described the birds singing in the bushes outside his window as chirpy little chaps, but today they annoyed him.

Normally Fred Fisher believed he had his ear to the ground, but the ground hadn't spoken. When he phoned his particular friend on the district council, his friend the editor of the *Gazette*, or his friend the President of Rotary they had been no help. Perhaps because he didn't know what to ask them, wanted rather to give them an opportunity to tell him something if they liked. Apparently they didn't like, either because they had nothing to tell or, more disturbingly, had something to hide.

What about his closest friend, he thought, adjusting his trousers to make space for an erection. Should he confide his worries to her? The idea didn't please him, making him supplicant rather than granter of favours. But as the days passed and her absence became more of a mystery he longed for her more urgently and wondered increasingly why, whenever he passed her house her upstairs curtains were drawn. Suppose, oh horror . . . But surely someone as efficient as Virginia would never make a mistake about the time in the month when she was incognito, as she described it. No doubt about it, he was in a double bind, a term he'd recently learned which seemed all too appropriate: on the one hand longing for her, on the other determined not to seem weak.

Meanwhile he should accept that some of his local landowning clients knew all about the double part he was having to play and didn't much like it. But it was more serious if villagers like Gertie Jumble as he called her, referring to the apparent source of her clothes, had rumbled him. Worst of all, if Virginia had discovered and was signalling her disappointment.

Restlessness drove him to visit the scene of the tragedy. Worth a try, since nothing else seemed to help. The path he took gave him another mystery to worry about. Passing Lorna Furnival's house on his way down into the valley he saw a police car parked outside. If only he could be a fly on the wall.

'Sit down then,' Lorna Furnival told them.

They remained standing, holding their uniform caps, which they'd politely removed at the door, across the front of their uniform trousers – rather like fig leaves, Lorna thought. Occasional voices crackled from small black boxes attached to their belts. She couldn't understand a word – and nor perhaps could they since they paid no attention, suggesting these were only meant to impress.

'What can I do for you?' Lorna sat herself in a basket chair which squeaked as it took her weight.

'We have a report,' the taller, apparently senior, officer said. 'Plants of a certain species have been discovered. . . . Perhaps you can help.'

'What plants?'

'To be frank, cannabis.' Using the word in front of a lady seemed to embarrass him.

'Oh that!' Lorna said. 'Smoke it all the time.'

They smiled uneasily.

'Anything else?'

'We understand you have been allowing certain young persons to occupy a caravan . . .'

'What has that to do with it?'

'We thought *you* might tell us.'

'Oh yes!' Lorna grew angry.

'There might be a criminal aspect, the dwelling being your property . . .'

'Are you threatening me?' It was only with the death of Bob Brandish that she'd realized how he and Sandra had come to interest her – were even perhaps becoming the children she'd never had. How annoying, she thought. At 73 such feelings should leave her alone.

'Go on, arrest me.' She stared fiecely at them.

They didn't smile. 'We may require a statement.'

'I've told you, I grow it, smoke it, eat it.' She'd been told that this was possible in buns.

'Mrs Furnival, we all like a joke.'

I doubt it, she thought, watching them get out their antiquated equipment – pen, lined writing block – and sit themselves at her table.

'We need to start with your name. "I Mrs Furnival"—'

'I shall want my solicitor to be present, of course.'

'Ah yes.' They still sat there, as if hoping something more convenient would happen. 'In that case . . .'

How stupid of me to tease them, she thought as she showed them out, even if they asked for it.

For the two officers it had been a frustrating morning, even before the interview with that old battleaxe whom they unwillingly respected. First there'd been Miss Wiggum, who wouldn't speak to them till school break, then would only discuss the charging of a driver of a metallic red car with attempted manslaughter.

On to the house of the accused, a certain Mr J. Cuff, who seemed not to be at home. So the senior officer had put out his hand towards the bell fixed to the iron railings at the same time peering through these to look for the described car, and had to jump backwards in shock as a huge Alsatian rushed towards him then rose on to its hind legs where it almost got a mouthful of his hand. At the same moment the junior officer thought he saw the curtain of an upper window stir.

Back in the village street they'd found the house of Mr Taylor, a possible witness named by the headmistress, but no amount of knocking and ringing would make him answer his door. A sudden clatter of what sounded like falling pots made them suspect that he might be in his garden shed and they cautiously circled this. Large white letters on its door read NO ENTRY, which wasn't anyhow possible because it seemed locked. Nor were there any windows but only a skylight. Cautiously the senior officer put his ear against the door and reported hearing rustling inside. Although his junior noticed an earwig attached to his sideburn he didn't report this.

Out manoeuvred by Mrs Furnival, they retreated to a lay-by where they parked as if to monitor the traffic, in fact to smoke.

'Looks like we got a bunch of Trappists,' the junior officer said.

The senior officer didn't answer, knowing that silence was the way to preserve respect. Presently he stubbed out his cigarette and gave his verdict. 'What would you expect, seeing they're all in it?'

Left in peace, Lorna had meanwhile opened again the book of village photographs she'd borrowed from Polly Langridge. It was a school group of the 1890s which fascinated her. There they all were, at least twice as many as today, in their pinnafores and high-buttoned jackets, all with their plans and hopes, all so alive and real, now all dead.

Opposite was a harvest group. Young men in straw hats and boots, these looking enormous since they were closer to the camera, a circular trophy on a tripod at their centre. The same was true of them, of course, but it was the children who moved her because they knew less and hoped more. What rubbish to think it had been a saner, more kindly world. Disease, endless pointless labour, early death – she was about to add bucolic stupidity, but wasn't so sure about that.

She shut the book and set out across her lawn towards her wood. How quiet it all seemed and gently warm, like a summer morning long ago, in a happier time, wonderful but sad and somehow unreal because . . . because, like those sepia images, she and the village she had loved would also soon be gone.

The wood was cooler as she descended through it, and now everywhere above her birds were flittering in sunlit branches. She smelt that moist woody smell which always pleased her, paused and breathed again – less good the second time. Here was the fallen oak on which she and

101

Harry would sometimes sit with a jug of Pimms, and after the second glass, he might talk about his business affairs and she would know that at least half of what he was saying was invention. Had he known that *she* knew? Usually not, she thought, and then, instead of looking past her at some dream she would unexpectedly discover him looking at her, as if surprised to find her listening. Had he also been her mischievous child?

She'd never blamed him, not even for what he probably thought of as his 'infidelities'. Why was sex so important? she thought, though less with anger than interest. He'd wanted a son, that was the easy explanation. Perhaps he'd wanted ultimately to leave her. Well he'd managed that and no mistake – accident be blowed. It was only his final desertion that she found hard to forgive. The truth was that Harry had been what her father called a cad. Just one glimpse of his carroty moustache had fixed that judgement firmly in her father's mind. It was probably because her father thought Harry a cad that she'd married him.

Now she descended alongside the green hose which she remembered helping Bob to lay, and for the first time wondered if people might think her responsible for the tragedy. Wasn't it she who'd brought these undesirable people to the village, lent them somewhere to live? What an appropriate punishment if her hose had caused the death of one of them.

Ahead and below she now saw their lichen-streaked caravan. Also saw people moving among the trees, but, increasingly short sighted, wasn't sure who they were. Ignoring them, she passed round the caravan – and had a shock: two people she didn't recognize. It took her several seconds to realize that this short-haired shrimp of a girl was Sandra, and the other one, equally short but massive, help-

ing her lift a baby into a kangaroo pouch, was Jack
Hawker's powerful daughter.

Taking Sandra by the wrist Lorna led her through trees to
the fertile patch of ground behind the old glass house. They
were certainly flourishing, eighteen inches high. Lorna
pointed at them with her stick.

'Some inquisitive men are interested.'

'Oh dear, I'm sorry.'

'My garden boy will be having a bonfire tomorrow.'

'Yes, of course.'

'I suppose you could stand in the smoke.' Lorna fought
against fondness for this innocent child. 'And take deep
breaths.'

She smiled.

'Should I join you?'

Back near the caravan, she saw no fewer than three
intruders gathered round the abandoned shaft's entry, as if
in consultation. She stopped and stared at them. Soon she'd
made all three look at her, a power she'd had since she was
a girl. The nearest, in shorts exposing bony knees, was
Michael Ranch, cuckolded husband of Virginia, people
assured her.

'Enjoying yourselves?' She considered mentioning that it
was *her* wood.

'Trying to resolve one or two inconsistencies,' the second
one told her – Ernest Boon, redundant civil servant,
ornithologist.

'We belong to the village history group.'

'Do you indeed!'

'Ancient water courses.'

Things grew clearer. Michael Ranch was holding a forked
stick. Water divining. She tried not to laugh at what was
probably anyway an excuse.

'It's been moving,' Ernest Boon told her.

'Twice, at least,' Michael Ranch said. 'Look.' He showed the palms of his hands. To Lorna they looked no whiter than those of any other 45-year-old welfare officer.

Now she recognized the third person, hopping towards her with raised knees as he found safe places for his feet. Fred Fisher, 'that dapper little twerp' as she remembered Harry once describing him. In Harry's time he'd been such an unimpressive adolescent as to be barely noticeable, a mere appendage to the person he lived with, poor old Professor Bobo.

'Morning, Lorna,' Fred called with cheeky familiarity. 'We've been wondering' – this was not true, but he would have liked it to be, to spread among the three of them her possible annoyance at finding them on her land – 'whether, on the night of the tragedy—'

'Fast asleep.'

'But weren't you—?'

'That's right. I was woken up.'

'Yes, of course,' Fred said, in a tone which meant, 'If that's your story there's not much I can do about it.' He gave several grunts, then continued, 'Ah well, "more things in heaven and earth" . . . as the bard said.'

'Certain possibilities we thought it appropriate to eliminate,' Michel Ranch said. 'Underground streams. Natural seepage. Before we can consider other possibilities.'

'Such as?'

She got no answer, as if each of them was waiting for one of the others. Were they implying that she should be able to guess? Lorna shrugged and set off for home.

They watched her climbing and occasionally stumbling among the trees, then, when she was far enough away, looked at each other and in turn raised their eyebrows.

'Well well!' Fred Fisher said.

It had been his good luck, Fred had thought, when he reached the abandoned hole in the ground to find these two already here. Or had it been? True they were eccentric enough for the water-divining explanation to be genuine, especially the tufted owl – his name for Ernest Boon – who was a pigeon fancier if ever there was one – Fred's shorthand for people, usually from suburban Manchester, who belonged to arcane clubs.

As for Michael Branch, Fred believed he had a civilized relationship with this inoffensive chap whose wife he was regularly laying – summed up in the phrase, 'Such things do happen'. Well, you never knew what a welfare officer might consider it his duty to investigate. While meeting either of them individually would not have made Fred anxious, finding them together was another matter, leading to the fear that they were plotting against him. Ah well, nothing to do, except behave as if he trusted and liked them if he wanted *them* to like *him*, and this above all was what Fred Fisher wanted.

Ernest Boon was far from sure that he dared to be any sort of a friend of Fred Fisher's. If ever he met and talked to him in a friendly way he was aware that he would have to report this to Tiffany quite differently. The sort of thing Tiffany would like him to tell her about the present meeting was the way Fred Fisher had ripped open one of his trouser legs on a bramble. He might improve this by remembering his bleeding shin. In fact, Ernest Boon was genuinely annoyed with Fred Fisher for arriving uninvited and discovering himself and Michael Branch busy with a genuine piece of investigation which, seen from the outside, might make them seem ridiculous.

Michael Branch, whose idea it had been, didn't think it

105

ridiculous, and was irritated with Fred Fisher for another reason. Since he was fond of Virginia he had from the first tried to treat her affair as a disease from which in due course she would recover. To betray hostility to someone she was apparently besotted about might delay her recovery. Secretly, however, he loathed this self-important little runt and for two years had been hoping for an opportunity for revenge.

What the three of them had in common was a suspicion that the death of Bob Brandish was a mystery which had not been fully explained.

Watching them from a distance, Briony Hawker knew something they would have liked to discover, which she doubted if they knew and which she was not going to tell them. Because the secret which Sandra had finally confessed to her was Sandra's, and there wasn't the smallest chance that she would ever pass it on.

'We must put a brave face on it,' actor-manager Fred Fisher told the dramatic society, assembled in the village hall to cast and perhaps even attempt a reading of the summer play.

'You could call it an act of defiance,' Fred Fisher continued. The company was uneasy at this, suspecting it was conceited.

The actor-manager had, in fact, already chosen a play, and since no one had answered his circular, had taken it as agreed: *King Lear*. 'It's ambitious,' he admitted, 'but I think you'll agree its appropriate.'

The majority seemed to agree, several faintly nodding though most of them not because they understood why it was appropriate but because they didn't want to look stupid to others who did.

Nor was there any doubt that the director would play the king – though Lorna Furnival would have questioned it if she could have been bothered. Things had been different when Professor Bobo had produced the village play, and she herself had taken parts, her large triangular nose adding flavour to a Lady Macbeth which some still remembered. Bobo, a man built on her own scale, had made them laugh, lumbering about the stage as he showed them what they should attempt. They had wanted to please him. He'd kept young Fred in his place, casting him as some comely – and scantily clothed – youth or fairy. Now, as self-appointed boss she found Fred Fisher even more irritating than as a chairman. Prancing about the stage, the only part she could imagine him playing was a Gilbert and Sullivan major general, could picture him leaping into the air, crossing and uncrossing his legs two or three times then landing in a heap. Others were worried that his small black beard would need much enlarging and bleaching for a convincing Lear.

Allocating other parts was not so simple. To have asked Geoff Riddle to play the Fool, for example, would have looked too much like type-casting. Nor to play Edmund because it would have drawn embarrassing attention to Geoff's squint when Edmund had his eyes plucked out. Some wit like Polly Langridge might have said it was an improvement.

'You like me to play the Fool?' Geoff Riddle asked.

Embarrassment . . . suppressed laughter.

'Jolly decent of you,' Ralph Gamble said. Ralph had brought Irma because he wanted her to play Cordelia. Years ago at his Seaford prep school Ralph remembered Brown Minor playing Cordelia. Other boys called him Sludge Brown, but Ralph had discovered that his real name was Andrew. For a whole Christmas term he'd longed to call him Andy. He would do it casually, during a rehearsal – the dress rehearsal perhaps, as he helped work the narrow sleeves of Cordelia's dress up Brown's small plump arms. 'You need some help, Andy?' Once he'd actually begun this prepared sentence, 'You need . . .' and come to a blushing halt. 'You must be hot in that,' he'd managed to substitute. Brown had given him a knowing look, but even if he'd understood what this meant he wouldn't have known what to do next. Nor could he be certain whether it was the following term or the one after that Mackintosh minor had arrived.

'First I'd like to explain my mehtod,' Fred Fisher said. 'Some people think Shakespeare difficult. I've known actors play a part for a whole run without the faintest idea what their lines mean. As for the plot . . . So what I do is translate every line into modern English. Then when you speak Shakespeare's lines you at least know what he's talking about.'

'Give us an example,' Tiffany Boon said. She – and most of the others – had heard Fred describe his method too often and had come prepared with a copy of the text borrowed from the public Library. Holding it up to the light she read:

> *'Who in the lusty stealth of nature take*
> *More composition and fierce quality*
> *Than doth, with a dull, stale, tired bed,*
> *Go to the creating a whole tribe of fops,*
> *Got 'tween asleep and wake?'*

Fred Fisher was shocked. Those exact lines had caught his attention in his own recent reading because, as the weeks passed and Virginia remained housebound, he'd become increasingly convinced that she was carrying *his* fop.

'Well, Tiffany, if you really want . . .'

As he hunted for some euphemistic explanation he remembered with some pride that exceptionally enjoyable event they'd shared, not ten feet away behind the village hall's stacking chairs on the district council's judo mattress, but also with a sinking stomach because its very splendour might have been their undoing. Furthermore, why had Tiffany, sharp little bitch, chosen this passage, if not because she'd guessed something?

'Not the easiest lines. Give me a day or two.'

'Look forward to it,' Tiffany said.

Casting Regan and Goneril might also be awkward, Fred had realized.

'You'll make a splendid Regan,' he told Briony Hawker.

'Would I?' Briony said sourly.

'Gertie, I'd like you for Goneril.'

'You would, would you?' Gertie Jones said threateningly.

Inevitable, Fred thought, that amateurs instead of seeing such parts as opportunities, would take being chosen as a comment on their own characters.

Still more difficult was Cordelia, since there were other candidates besides Irma, each with a supporter. Ernest Boon had hoped that Tiffany might be chosen and so acquire the idea that there was no need to be so consistently fierce. Briony had brought Sandra and hoped she would get the part because she was becoming a problem. At any moment of the day Briony would discover her sobbing for no reason that Briony could understand.

Fred made all three Cordelias mount the stage and start at the third line of page six. 'Nothing my Lord.' This gave him the chance each time to answer, 'Nothing shall come of nothing. Speak again,' with magnificent resonance, in contrast to their timid whispers, a response which caused

Sandra, who read last to start to sob once more.

'Splendid,' Fred congratulated her, though he was think-ing about something else. Surely, yes surely he could offer Virginia Ranch the part, so giving him the excuse for calling at Meadowsweet to offer it to her.

'I must think it over,' he told them. 'You're each splendid in your different ways.' His plan had put him in such excel-lent humour that he barely noticed that no one smiled.

'Didn't we orter be doing something contemporary like?'

Astonished silence. Heads turned to see who had spoken. Though Geoff Riddle sat staring ahead in silence it seemed increasingly likely that it was he.

'I was under the impression we'd agreed . . .' Fred began.

'Who was that what agreed?' No doubt now that this was Geoff Riddle.

'Are you suggesting a Terrence Rattigan for example?' Fred said, scoring what Lorna Furnival considered a contemptible point.

Many were by now realizing that something embarrassing had happened and beginning to explain to their neighbours that the director was being challenged. Miss Mary Wiggum told Evan Mullins that contemporary costumes would be much easier. Admiral Hawker remembered how as a small boy he'd enjoyed playing Peter Pan – and went purple in the face with embarrassment at this memory. Ernest Boon told Mrs Volga that it was for her to suggest Chekhov, to prevent him suggesting it himself and being snubbed by Tiffany. Michael Ranch told Ernest Boon that Shaw had only written *Joan of Arc* to prevent Drinkwater ruining the subject, though he himself preferred *The Apple Cart*. Lorna Furnival said they'd had a village procession for the coronation, but no one was sure which coronation she meant. At the back of the hall Joan Wodge was trying to say something about Morris dancing, but was so small it was difficult to see or hear her.

Fred Fisher let the chatter continue till it dribbled to a stop, then asked Geoff Riddle to be more precise about what he proposed.

'Up to you.' Geoff muttered.

'You saying it would be about us?' Polly Langridge said.

'I understand,' Fred said. What he saw in fact was an escape. 'You're suggesting we compose something ourselves. So who is going to write this original work?'

Silence. Yes, if he stayed calm and gave them a little guidance he would surely make them see sense.

It was growing dark before Fred drew the meeting skilfully to a close. 'We're a democratic company,' he told them, and proposed the establishment of a small committee 'to thrash out this whole matter.'

It was during his concluding remarks that he became aware of sounds which seemed to come from the back of the hall. He'd been the last to hear these because whoever was making them seemed to be intentionally timing them to coincide with his own words. Only now that he heard one in isolation. Laughter? Surely not. But that was what it sounded like. Mocking laughter.

'Did you speak?' he called into the shadows.

'What me!'

'Who are you?'

'You know me.'

By now they all did.

'I don't think I have the pleasure.'

'You soon will.'

No one knew whether Joseph Cuff had been there all the time or had just arrived. They saw him now, a thick, short shape, near the rear entrance, his heavily freckled face almost invisible.

'I must ask you to leave, whoever you are.'

'You can ask till you're stupid. It's a public hall.'

'This is a private society.'

'Private society! You know what you can do with your private society . . .'

He stopped. A tall, gangling figure was advancing on him. 'Get out,' Ralph Gamble shouted.

'I'll go when I please.'

'Now.'

Forty-five years ago, Ralph had occasionally watched school-boxing matches, but only once as far as he could remember taken part in one, the result a four-hour nose bleed. Nevertheless, he now raised his hands, left fist forward, in a parody of a nineteenth-century pugilist.

Joseph Cuff also raised his fists and began to dance about, swaying his head from side to side, jabbing the air. 'Come on, hit me, what you waiting for?'

Shouts and confusion then a thumping fall followed by gasps and loud groans. Several people took hold of other people – though not always the intended ones. Others tried to pull the two fighters apart. Only later were they able to help each other create an agreed version of what had happened. Ralph Gamble, it seemed, had aimed with his left fist at Cuff's head and Joseph Cuff had used his left leg to knee Ralph in the testicles.

CHAPTER SEVEN

A DOG'S LIFE

'I'M a dangerous man to cross.' 'Don't trifle with me.' Joseph Cuff's fury was supported by slogans which churned in his head. If they block the road with an idiotic march, it isn't his fault.

All right, he'd been in a mood that morning. His mother could induce in Joseph Cuff a fury which made his heart thump at a frightening rate and sweat break out on his hairy arms. That morning she'd been sick into her breakfast cereals. On purpose. Perhaps he shouldn't have tried her with bran flakes. Before he could clear up the foul mess he'd needed to spend ten minutes pacing up and down his drive. Out there he'd found his hands convulsively opening and closing, as if squeezing something tighter and tighter.

As for that threatening letter – what did they expect? Then sending the police. Typical that his mother should refuse to come down and ask what they wanted, when he'd wisely decided not to be at home and hidden the car in the garage.

They hadn't come back, that was a good sign. So what

else should he do except carry on as if he'd nothing to answer for? Take part in their pathetic play acting, and so get charged with assault? Of course not, seeing it was he who'd been assaulted. Three days later, Joseph Cuff's alsatian, Gideon, died. The shot had been fired at close range, but bits of brain and bone were scattered about the drive. There must, in fact, have been a second shot, fired while he lay jerking about on the ground, still with a recognizable head, because the gravel had been scraped by his paws and contained lead pellets. And fired some hours before he'd arrived home, seeing how congealed the blood had become. It was to be expected that his mother would not admit to having heard anything, but why had no one else, when there were houses only fifty yards away?

The most obvious assassin was, of course, Ralph Gamble.

'Bastard got me in the privates,' Ralph said, hunched in a leather armchair, wrapped in a dressing-gown.

'So I will not be – how you say – getting my onions?' Irma Svenson asked him, making a joke of a serious matter.

'I tell you, he got mine.'

Irma had been getting her onions with enjoyable regularity, so much so that a mutual tenderness was threatening to succeed lust. One morning she'd found a love note on her breakfast muesli and given Ralph a big kiss.

Just when things were going so well, Ralph thought bitterly.

His humiliating injury was ample motive for revenge. He was also known to have a case full of guns. But some said that he surely wouldn't have done it since he would so obviously be the suspect. And there were other suspects. He and Geoff Riddle were known friends. Didn't Geoff help Ralph rear his pheasants? And though Geoff was not a member of Ralph's shooting syndicate, he was known to possess what he described as 'my old musket', a hammer-action 12 bore, which he occasionally fired in the direction of a distant flock of pigeons. For secrecy, Geoff kept this undeclared weapon just inside his barn, behind a mangle shredder, unused for many years. Though some doubted whether Geoff, with his squint, could even have hit a large dog at point-blank range.

It seemed that the police had yet other suspicions, if there was any truth in what Mrs Volga told Lorna Furnival, almost the only person who would listen properly to her.

'I haf new friend.'

'You have!' Lorna was again at her easel in the church-yard. She was suspicious. Surely everyone had known for months about Mrs Volga and Mr Taylor.

'He is most interesting man.'

'Keeps it to himself.'

'He is having so much a sad life. His wife runs away with a man in a wheelchair.'

'*In* the wheelchair?'

'His garden is all is left of him. Now he has new trouble.'

'Yes?'

'A man stare at him.'

Lorna dabbed more colour on some vulgar pink gerani-ums, lately planted by the Revd Charlie Sage around the church porch.

'He does not say one word. Just stands and stares. Would you like that?'

'Probably not.'

'Sometimes he laughs.'

'Who does?'

'My friend is so frightened. Soon he will not dare to go to his garden. Then he will die.'

'We're all going to do that.'

'From grief.'

'So what's it all about?'

'Some policemen are asking him questions. Has he seen something?'

Lorna began to make guesses. The harasser was a mystery, but the disruption of the school march, vividly described to her by Polly Langridge, though in fact Polly hadn't seen it, had probably occurred within sight of Mr Taylor's garden and the police might be looking for witnesses. There was also the killing of the dog. The idea of Mr Taylor as a dog killer might seem absurd, but you never knew what ideas the police might have.

She'd seen a pair of them going through the school gates the other day, as if looking for the headmistress.

They had found her, as their colleagues previously had, in a state of distress. Sitting at her desk, her heaving bosom had suggested to one of them, whose hobby was sailing, an ocean swell after a gale – seven minor heaves, followed by one huge one. At 3.30 that afternoon she'd found Justin and Howard Prone in the playground stuffing thistles up Elsie Patch's knickers.

'Whatever are you doing, you horrid boys?'

'Disinfectin' her, miss.'

'*What!*'

'Weren't it her give it to us – the squits?'

'Oh, what rubbish. If anybody gave it to anyone, *you* gave it to *her*.'

The thistles themselves had been easily rescued in spite of Elsie's howls, but unfortunately some of the prickles remained embedded in her bottom. Justin and Howard watched the operation with pained innocence. 'If she knowd what we done for her,' Justin told Howard, loud enough for Miss Wiggum to hear.

Now Elsie's parents arrived, Mrs Patch to scream at Miss

Wiggum and remove Elsie, Mr Patch to threaten legal action. Shirley Prone arrived soon afterwards and also screamed. 'Leads them on, that's what that little hussie does!'

Patiently the officers calmed Miss Wiggum and laboriously translated into police English the same account of the reckless driving of one Mr Cuff she had given to their colleagues but insisted on repeating. Their suggestion that she might know something about the killing of a pedigree dog she barely seemed to hear.

'Mr Cuff's dog,' the senior officer said softly.

'Those who live by the sword . . .' Miss Wiggum said, but went no further and there was a short silence.

'So when will you charge him?' she asked, squashing their attempt to change the subject.

The constables didn't answer.

'You mean he won't be charged? Is that what you're saying?' Miss Wiggum's bosom began to heave again.

Meanwhile Polly Langridge, excited by reports of the boxing match, as it was now described, at the village hall, went waddling down Chestnut Lane to see if she could discover anything interesting. She was rewarded by a glistening red car, parked outside Mr Fisher's house. Noticing that his front door was ajar she thought of a question she needed to ask him, pushed gently and stepped inside. Standing in the narrow passage which Fred called his hall she heard raised voices.

'I warn you, I'm dangerous.'

'You don't have to tell me.' That was Mr Fisher, talking in his funny way.

'I got London friends. You could be sorry.'

Polly Langridge withdrew, softly closing the front door, adding Mr Fisher's name to the list of those who might have killed that poor dog.

In his front room, Fred Fisher tried to suppress frightening thoughts. Friends in London meant the East End. Disconnected brake cables, petrol bombs through his letter box, anonymous death threats. 'Oh, sorry, old boy.' He'd been so distracted that he'd accidentally knocked down one or two of his children who had arrived to chase each other round the room. 'I say there, cheer up.' First Jamie howled then Sally at a more hysterical pitch as both ran to look for their mother.

What most astonished Fred was his own stupidity. Could he really have invited this man to drop in with the idea that a friendly chat and an exchange of apologies would calm him?

'The problem is,' he'd begun, 'my memory of what happened may not be precisely the same as other people's. So bringing a case for assault against Mr Gamble might not be as simple as you think.'

'You admit he was responsible?'

'Certainly not,' Fred said, realizing that the man might not be talking about the unfortunate incident at the village hall and the possibility of a charge of assault but about the killing of his dog. How English, he thought, temporarily forgetting that he didn't usually think of Mr Cuff as properly English, to let the death of a dog come before a charge of assault, not to mention the mysterious drowning of a human being.

'I'll see what I can do,' Fred suggested, an offer he'd found could suit a variety of awkward requests. Though perhaps not this one judging by the unpleasant way the man continued to stare at him.

'You think I'll let this rest? It won't be the last you hear.'

But Fred was hardly listening because something had

suddenly clicked in his mind. Was this aggressive fellow being too keen about the dog? Suppose he knew something about that other tragedy. True, this didn't fit with other suspicions he'd recently been having; for example, why had those two water diviners been so keen to establish some natural cause for the lad's death which, as far as he knew, hadn't directly affected either of them?

Later that morning, Fred Fisher decided what he must do. The drama society hadn't definitely rejected *Lear*. It was quite reasonable that he should offer Cordelia to Virginia.

A long pause when he rang her bell, long enough for him to assure himself that on a weekday her husband would be at work. Michael Ranch was not at work and now opened the door.

'Oh hallo.'

'Good morning.'

'Glad I found you at home,' Fred said, already congratulating himself on his calmness when faced with this unfortunate development and the clever explanation he'd at once thought of. 'Been wondering about what conclusions you reached. Your investigations. Down in the woods – you remember? About water. . . ?'

The longer he blundered on the more the man's silence disturbed him.

'Ah well, no doubt all will become clear as mud, in God's good time. One other thing, while I'm here. You know we're planning to stage *Lear*. Would you mind if I suggested to your good wife she play Cordelia?'

'I suggest you bugger off,' Michael Ranch said.

'Oh well,' Fred said, 'if that's the way you see it.' But he didn't at once obey, hunting for a better note on which to end this unfortunate meeting. Finding none, he said, 'Well, bye for now,' turned and retreated between the lines of perfectly trimmed aubretia. As he went, he was aware that the man hadn't shut his door but was watching him every step to the garden gate. Worse, turning to shut this and glancing back at the house he distinctly saw drawn curtains above the porch stir then move slightly apart.

Gradually on Fred Fisher's hundred-yard walk home, his dismay was replaced by amazement. He'd never heard the man talk like that, or imagined he was capable of it. Which led to suspicion. Perhaps there was indeed something in poor old Michael's behaviour, which the naughtiness of his wife didn't explain.

That night Truffle, Bob Brandish's lurcher, died. Soon after Sandra blew out the candle he started to whine. 'Needs a crap,' Briony said, and shoved him out. Next morning they found him lying stiff and cold beside Lorna's derelict glass house. Certainly the wound Gideon had given him had never healed, but that could hardly have killed him.

'Perhaps he ate something,' Sandra said.

'But what?' Briony said.

'Perhaps he was missing Bob. I think he'd like a funeral pyre.'

Briony seemed less than enthusiastic.

'I'm sure Foxglove would understand.'

For an hour they collected timber, then for half an hour tried to light it, and eventually it burned fiercely, a light wind carrying a repulsive smell up through Lorna's wood to the village street. Still Truffle wouldn't burn and as dusk fell they dug him a grave, though a shallower one than Briony would have liked because it soon began to fill with water.

CHAPTER EIGHT

A LONG SHOT

FOR a week they had had summer, the sort of summer which came rarely but expanded in memory to become summer after remembered summer. Lorna Furnival scrumpled her botched geraniums, collapsed her easel, slammed shut her camping stool and started for home.

Tonight it was so still that she could hear the rooks far down the valley, still squabbling as they arrived to roost. Down there a pigeon cooed, a wood pigeon, not one of these pretty little doves. More than any other sound, it took her back to long-ago summer holidays. The swifts had come back too, squealing above her as she painted, endlessly circling the church spire. Knowing what might happen, she had wondered if they would come this year. Harry had once told her that for the first four years of their lives they never settled – flew continuously, eating, sleeping and making love on the wing. Reaching her back lawn she met what she had hoped for – the dense scent of stock. There it was, luminous in the dusk, all the way to the edge of her wood.

Lorna did not sleep.

At dawn she made herself look out of her bedroom window. Just to make sure there wasn't another empty white envelope, she thought, and laughed at herself. These days she moved heavily from room to room in the house, but her mind raced. Several times she stood in a doorway wondering why she'd arrived there. She opened her back door and looked out across her lawn. Wouldn't it be better to sell now and go away with things to remember instead of enduring their slow destruction – grinding machines in the valley, the crash of falling trees, then the endless roar of traffic where there had once been a kind of peace?

> *Oh that I were brisk and spry*
> *To give him that for which to cry.*

The lines went on and on in her head but she could remember no more. Not even whether it was Belloc or Chesterton. Though she knew who she was thinking about.

'Up with the lark,' Fred Fisher said, opening his front door to her. 'Come right in.'

Lorna Furnival scowled. His front passage reeked of lavender spray, presumably hiding something worse.

'Coffee? I'm sure we can rustle up a mug.'

Lorna told him about the empty envelope.

'I am sorry,' Fred Fisher said.

'Are you? Why? Do you know something?'

'No no, just sorry for you. Understand how you must feel. Nasty things anonymous letters.'

'But there wasn't a letter.'

'So you tell me. Funny thing and no mistake.'

'You suggesting it's some sort of joke?'

'Possibly.' Did my best to calm the old bird, he thought, rehearsing how he'd report this tiresome intrusion to his mistress, if she was ever that again.

'Perhaps a comment on how little we've achieved?'

Fred Fisher shrugged. 'Terribly careless nowadays, with other people's property. I've seen a carpenter (it was a safe anecdote, one of his usual) spraying more nails into the surrounding grass than he ever hit with his hammer. Too lazy to pick 'em up. He wasn't paying for them . . .'

'I've no idea what you're talking about.'

'Funny, nor have I. ' He gave an apologetic grin, hoping for one in return but not getting it. 'To be serious . . .'

'About time,' Lorna thought.

'Would it count as harassment? Just about anything does nowadays.'

'You suggesting I should see my solicitor?'

'Yes, you do that,' Fred said, and regretted too late the relief in his tone. 'Need a lift?' He knew she had no car, had never replaced the one in which Harry had come to his unfortunate end. 'Tell me when and I'll run you over.'

'Let's say now.'

'Oh ah, oh well . . .'

But when Fred Fisher phoned it turned out that the gentleman, as Fred described him, was in court all day.

So it was the next afternoon they set out. The bright blue sky of the previous day had clouded, but it was even hotter. The air was tropically moist. Fred Fisher, jacket discarded, but with tie and cuff links, sweated under his armpits. Lorna's hip ached, as it usually did in such weather.

Vivian Mountjoy, of Alberry and Mountjoy, was a gentle-man she found it difficult not to dislike. For a year and a half, while he'd sorted out the confusion in which Harry had left his affairs, he'd made his opinion of Harry increas-ingly clear without ever risking an offensive word. There he sat, the flaps of his jacket overlapping his swivel chair's seat so making himself and the chair seem like a single sculpture. His smooth grey hair shone in the sunlight which came through his office's mock Tudor windows. His smile came unexpectedly, as if he'd almost forgotten it, but disappeared as quickly.

'The letter isn't important,' she told him. 'I want a general opinion on my legal rights.' It was the only reason she'd come. 'They're my trees they'll be felling, on my land.'

'I seem to recall that on the last occasion we discussed the matter . . .'

'Oh yes, I know we've been over it before. But not when it was so urgent. Surely there must be something I can do.'

Longish pause. 'Nothing legal, I fear.' Smile. No smile. 'Didn't I hear that someone had already tried something of that sort? With unfortunate consequences.'

Vivian Mountjoy moved one of his plump, pink hands, laid out like an animal's paws on his desk, and made a note, but stayed welded to his chair.

Her difficulty was that she liked his precision. Her grandfather, her mother's father, known as Friar Tuck perhaps because of his girth, had been a lawyer. Lorna remembered how asking Father John questions was not like questioning other grown ups. The pause before he answered went on so long she would want to skip about. Sometimes she did, and he would observe her skipping while still considering his advice. Partly she skipped with impatience, but more because she loved the way he was thinking seriously about her question. Then her father would interrupt with his own answer or a different question and she would realize that Father John was no longer going to take so much trouble about his own answer.

'If I discover anything . . .' Again that momentary smile.

'Any useful tips?' Fred Fisher asked, collecting her to

drive her home. He'd taken the opportunity to visit a property dealer he advised in the High Street.

Lorna grunted.

'Can't say I was hopeful,' Fred said, 'to be honest,' he
added, and pretended not to notice the sharp look this
provoked.

Outside her house stood a flashing police car. 'Ho ho, we
have visitors,' Fred said. 'Expected?'

'Not by me.' They were Big and Little again, looking as if
they'd already knocked at her door and, getting no answer,
were considering who to frighten next.

'Sure I can't be of any help?' Fred said.

'Hold my stick while I get out.'

As soon as she'd managed it – horrid things, cars – she
advanced on them. They smiled at her, as if their self-esteem
had recently been improved by bashing the odd protester.
But perhaps she was hard on them. She'd always been
liable, she knew, to lapse into sarcasm. Today she was
almost pleased to see them.

'Mrs Furnival?'

'Who would you think?' They couldn't help annoying
her. She came past them and opened her door. Without a
word they followed her in. There was something offen-
sively familiar about their silence, as if they were saying,
'We all know what this is about, and this time we're sure
you won't be difficult.' She led them into her dining-room
and stood on the far side of the polished oak table, propped
on her stick, keeping them standing on the other side. Her
aching hip was putting her in the right mood for policemen.

'Might we ask a few questions?'

'I can't stop you.'

'How did you first become aware of the unfortunate
event?'

'Which event? Haven't there been rather a lot?'

'The ambulance received the call out at 10.33 p.m. Presumably you had been previously alerted—'

'Screams.'

'Ah yes. That would be about. . . ?'

'How could I possibly know what it was about?'

'Of course, but the time?'

'Your guess is as good as mine.'

'You had no watch? Perhaps you saw a clock?'

She laughed at him, then forgave him. 'That's right.'

'And previous to that you were. . . ?'

'In bed.'

'Ah yes.' More such private details weren't necessary, he implied. 'So you rose . . . ?'

'You don't imagine I could stay asleep with that racket right outside my window.' In fact it had come from the far edge of her lawn. Caught in her torch beam, the girl had seemed stuck there, unable to decide whether or not to come closer.

'And you became aware. . . ?'

Lorna missed several questions, staring at him but thinking of something else. There the wretched girl had stood, making that mindless noise, like some awful wind-up toy. Anger, was what Lorna had felt. Even when she'd reached her it had been a minute or two before she could make her stop screaming and explain. Something was full of water. Because she already knew what they'd been doing down there in her wood, she'd begun to guess what might have happened.

'Why are you so sure?' Lorna had asked the girl.

Half-lit by her torch, she'd no longer screamed, but her teeth were chattering and she was shivering from her shoulders to her knees.

126

'How do you know he's down there, not out poaching perhaps?'

'He is,' Sandra had said.

And Lorna had believed her. Even if she'd doubted it she'd had no choice but to hurry to the house and phone, then stand with the girl at the roadside. That was when she'd started to shout insults at them.

'At least twenty-five minutes,' Lorna told the policemen.

'Would you say the young lady appeared distressed?'

'What do you imagine?'

Again she could hardly attend because something more worrying had come back to her. She seemed to remember that as she crossed the lawn she'd heard that faint gurgle which the water made in the hose pipe when it was flowing. Or had she? She knew the sound well, had often heard it when she walked on her lawn, telling her that down there they were washing or cooking – or watering their hemp. She seemed to remember hearing it on that night as well. But was it likely that she'd have noticed such a thing when she'd been hurrying to reach the screaming girl, then back to the house to phone? The more she tried to attach the sound to that particular night the less sure she became.

One thing was certain: she mustn't show by her abstraction that she was hiding something. She was impatient for them to go before she said something stupid. At last they did and she watched their car drive out of sight.

Ten minutes later she'd reached the point where, looking down through her trees, she could see the lichen-streaked caravan – caravanning, another of Harry's dreams. Someone short and broad was standing outside its door, in black jeans and bulging black jacket – the admiral's daughter, of course, who, without asking leave, had apparently taken up residence in her caravan. Lorna had been amused

127

by this bold cheek.

She waved. Briony Hawker didn't wave.

Though she had always liked Briony, approved of her defiant acceptance of her plainness, she was annoyed to find her apparently guarding Sandra. It was to Sandra she wanted to talk, on her own. She'd descended several more awkward steps before she stopped again and, called down 'Just to warn you, our friends the police have been visiting again.' Still getting no answer she began to climb back the way she'd come.

The day had grown hotter. Not a breath of wind. Tiredness was affecting her balance and, as she reached her lawn, she stumbled, would have fallen but for her stick. She forced herself on, afraid that if she stopped she might not start again, reached her dining-room sideboard and poured herself a brandy and soda.

That was better, helped her to realize that it wasn't the mystery of the boy's death that should be concerning her but its consequences. Long ago she ought to have seen that there was just a faint possibility that what he'd failed to do when alive his death might achieve. Lorna phoned for a taxi.

It was four o'clock when she reached the council chambers.

'Sir Rupert Brandish?'

The receptionist – skinny with bleached white hair and a pink jewel in her nose – said she would find out. 'Do you have an appointment?'

'I do not.' She could imagine his secretary suggesting a date next month. By then goodness knows what would have happened, not least to her courage.

'I'm afraid he's in a meeting.'

'Are you?'

128

'What? Oh!' She giggled.

'How long will it last?'

'You never know. Anyway after that I'm afraid he's busy.'

'Well I'm not so I'll wait.'

'He usually goes home about five.'

'Well, if he does, explain to him that he'll find me waiting for him in the morning.' And don't tell me he's going on holiday, she thought of adding.

Though waiting was the last thing she wanted because it gave her time to realize that she'd been wanting to meet the man with no prepared plan, just the hope that the right words would somehow come to her. But what words could be right? How could she suggest to him that he was responsible for his son's death, let alone that he should make amends by supporting the boy's cause? Put so clearly, what she'd thought an hour ago to be possible now seemed so ridiculous that she wished she'd never come.

'Mrs Furnival? Do come up.'

Up she followed him, to a surprisingly small room, largely filled by a desk, at which he chose not to sit, instead offering her a chair and sitting opposite her in another. The fact that there was only just room for them increased Lorna's sense that she was being trapped.

'Good of you to come. We meet too seldom.'

In fact hardly ever. At one time she used to see him at the sort of parties she no longer went to. Dark-haired then; 'cunning' was the word she might have used to describe him. Now 'tired' seemed better. Presumably he'd already been grey at his son's funeral and she'd not noticed.

'What can I do for you?'

It was a trap all right, the charm trap. She wanted to say, it's not what you can do but what you *will* do.

'Nothing, I expect.'

'Well that saves me explaining what I usually have to explain to visitors. They come thinking I have power and influence. I'm afraid it's not true.'

The calculated modesty left Lorna slightly sickened. So did the whole act, not least because it failed to explain why his son had revolted against him. Perhaps it was a convenient illusion to believe that anyone was real and not just a bundle of unrelated responses.

'I should have told you how sorry I was . . .' she said and, hearing it back, was annoyed at how gruff it sounded.

He said nothing, just gently shook his head, no longer looking her in the eyes, but in the region of the stomach.

'The truth is . . .' she began, but how pompous that sounded. 'The truth is, I liked your son. Why? Because he was asking himself questions we never dare ask. Trying to do something instead of moan and grumble. Easy for me, you say. I wasn't his father.'

He'd stopped shaking his head but she had no idea whether he was still listening, or just blocking the bad mannered things she was saying.

'You think I was responsible because I gave him somewhere to live. I wouldn't blame you.'

'Mrs Furnival, I think it would be best if we didn't discuss these matters.'

'Yes, of course. But you see it has occurred to me that we should do something for him now he's gone. And that you're the only person who could have the slightest chance of doing it. No, don't answer.'

There was a pause in which both of them seemed to realize that they had strayed into unfortunate territory and didn't know how to escape.

'I'm just a rude old woman. I should never have come.'

She staggered to her feet, stumbled towards the door but

not quickly enough to prevent him taking her by the elbow, helping her down those stairs to the hall. Here he let her go, but remained watching her as if she was a boat he'd set adrift which might or might not float.

'Thank you for coming,' he said.

And, of course, he'd won because she'd been left with no idea whether he honestly meant it or was lapsing instinctively into charm.

Around seven that evening she heard the first roll of thunder. A distant rumble, far across the valley, but such a long one that at first she thought it was yet another of those planes reversing its engines. It was from this direction that she still occasionally heard the cuckoo, though later and further away each year. In those summers there'd been grasshoppers in the meadows and glow-worms in the banks of the lanes. She tottered to the sideboard. She deserved what Harry would have called 'the other half.' Around midnight they would still be having the other half It was one of their jokes, funnier the more they had.

Another distant rumble, no nearer, but even longer, as if several rolls had merged into one. Down there towards the coast they were having a storm and no mistake. She looked up sharply. Surely that had been her doorbell.

Standing on her doorstep in the dusk, Ernest Boon, round faced with those white tufts above his ears, looked more than usually owl-like. Once before she remembered him surprising her when they'd been standing together in the churchyard discussing the weather and he'd seen an inoffensive black cat slinking between the tombstones. Stopping in mid-sentence, his face had distorted with anger and he'd started to hiss at it then dashed in pursuit. She led him to her sitting-room.

'Sherry?'

Though he followed her he didn't seem to hear.

'Something's happened,' he said. 'Tiffany. My wife. She's gone.'

'Gone?'

'To New Zealand. Auckland, to be precise. Our son lives there.'

'I suppose he invited her.'

'I've no idea.'

'You mean she didn't say she was going? Or leave a note? People usually do.' When they commit suicide, she'd been about to add.

'I haven't found one.'

'Hmm,' Lorna said. 'You're sure it's New Zealand?'

'Where else?'

'Frinton,' Lorna suggested. His blank stare seemed to invite teasing, but he didn't seem to hear.

'She said this village was a disgusting place.'

'Meaning?'

'Immorality. Giving the part to that whore. Those were her words.'

'What part?'

'Cordelia. Tiffany had set her heart on it.'

'I don't understand.'

'He's sent us all a note saying he's going to offer it to Mrs Ranch. Virginia.'

'Oh, the play,' Lorna said. 'I thought that was cancelled.'

'So did we all.'

'Surely that's not enough to make someone go to New Zealand.'

'You don't know Tiffany.'

'Probably not.'

'He says it's nice there. Our son.'

'Even so . . .'

'She's always secretly wanted to go on the stage. I blame myself for not supporting her.'

'Rubbish,' Lorna said. 'Anyway presumably you do support her.'

'Oh materially, yes. Not in the other ways I suppose.'

'Well, if she's gone she's gone. I don't see there's much you can do about it. Nor me, for that matter.'

'I just suppose I wanted to tell someone.' He leant forward from the chair he'd sat on the edge of and stared at the carpet.

'Funny,' he began, and seemed to hesitate, then with an effort went on, 'us being in the same boat.'

'*Us*? What do you mean?'

'Deserted.'

The awful truth came to Lorna. He was trying to drag her into his own world of the defeated. She would have liked to drive him out, if she'd had the strength.

'I can't imagine what makes you describe my husband's accident in that way.'

Worse still, he was now staring knowingly at her.

'You see, Mrs Furnival, where I used to work I had access to certain files . . .'

'Which you read.'

'I'm sorry if—'

'Are you? I doubt it.'

They were silent; staring at each other, each astonished at what they had said, each wondering how to return to civilized behaviour.

Unable to devise a better solution she crossed to her sideboard.

'Would you prefer brandy?'

'Thanks.'

They sipped cautiously.

Presently she saw Ernest Boon take out his handkerchief and surreptitiously dab his eyes.

Tears. It came back to her, of course. Poor Lord Lundy's aunt.

An empty wish alas for she
Was blind and nearly 93.

Did it mean that *she* had another twenty years? Lorna thought And did she want them?

Now the man was putting his handkerchief into a pocket. 'You'd think something like this would bring us all closer together,' he said, and sniffed.

'Like what?' Lorna said. 'Oh, the motorway. Well, that's one thing which never occurred to me.'

CHAPTER NINE

ON THE JOB

'YOU covered that lad's drowning,' the editor told Keith Haresnip.

Young Haresnip nodded.

'There may be developments.'

'You've heard something?'

'In a job like ours we must cultivate the local constabulary. I flatter myself that's one thing I've never neglected. They may be a corrupt bunch of under-achievers but every now and again they drop you a useful crumb. If they don't drop it on our plate they'll drop it on someone else's.'

'Who'd pay them more,' Keith Haresnip suggested, with a bold cynicism which he by no means trusted.

'Did I say that?' his editor demanded, staring fiercely at Haresnip, which Haresnip knew was as close to approval as he could expect.

'See what you can dig up, young man.'

Which would offer him a faint chance of glimpsing again those knee and elbow pads. Keith Haresnip had a fantasy of making love to her while they – but nothing else – were strapped to her, and hurried away, controlling an impulse to relieve his passion in the Gents – although he believed he could have managed that without audible groaning, as the sports editor was in the habit of doing around mid-morning – no no, his love was not to be wasted so crudely.

The cab dropped him in front of a brutally ugly row of concrete council houses labelled Keats Villas. As good as anywhere, Keith Haresnip thought, since he planned a surreptitious approach, alert for material as he went. Already an unexpected source had arrived in the form of a cluster of urchins playing outside Number 2.

'Who're *you*?' one cried.

'Why aren't *you* in school?' he countered.

'Teacher's ill, teacher's ill,' they sang.

'I'm the press,' he told them.

'He's the press what does press-ups,' one yelled.

'He's the reporter what reports yer,' yelled another, as they scampered away into a clump of laurels set in brick-hard mud, so clearly drooping in the heat that even Haresnip – not brought up anywhere near a garden – recognized their distress. The floppy limbs of the last child to disappear suggested imbecility.

Now he noticed a skinny woman in the open doorway of what was presumably their home. She wore a sagging, once-white T-shirt and propped herself by one shoulder against the doorpost, where she periodically disappeared behind tobacco smoke.

'From the *Gazette*,' he explained to her. 'Those yours?'

'Fuckin' are,' Shirley Prone admitted, shifting a bony hip and half closing her eyes against the smoke.

Behind the woman, almost invisible because of the bright outdoor sunlight, Haresnip thought he saw another figure, had the impression of a long pale face. He also noticed an

136

immaculate, cream-white Peugeot, looking as if it had strayed into bad company among rusty Fiestas and dented Volvos in the nearby parking line.

'I suppose you've heard the news,' he tried cunningly.

Shirley Prone sucked deeply and blew. When asked for something it was her instinct not to give it away cheaply, especially when she didn't know what it was.

'About the motorway.'

'They got what's coming to them,' Shirley Prone said. It was also her instinct to hint mysteriously when she had nothing to reveal.

'Who would *they* be?'

'The whole fuckin' shower. Well, wouldn't you?'

Keith Haresnip floundered – then was inspired. 'May I quote you?'

'Please yourself,' Shirley Prone said. 'Here, you, come outer there,' she screamed, setting off towards the laurels. Didn' I tell yer ter keep outer them?'

Haresnip approached the open doorway and spoke to the pale face which was all he could see. It belonged to Michael Ranch, husband of Virginia, social worker, who had secured Mrs Prone and her multi-fathered family as one of his cases.

'Would you share the lady's views?'

No answer.

'Do they belong to you?' Some of them could now be seen peering curiously from among those laurels.

'Certainly not.'

'But you live here?'

'Wrong again.'

Oh dear, thought Haresnip, things were not going well. The mother now returned and began to discuss the man who was not their father. 'You don't imagine he'd be bringing up that lot in a dump like this?' Then, turning to Haresnip, 'Go on, you tell them. They might listen to you. I can't say anything because of late payments and likely conviction.'

'Eviction,' the tall, pale man corrected her. Michael Ranch found Shirley Prone's vocabulary strangely erotic, but less so than the way her T-shirt sagged below her skinny collar bones.

'Nice talking to you,' Haresnip said and set off down a dusty footpath which led to the village street. As soon as he reached this he met a stout woman in ample, floral print carrying a shopping bag – Polly Langridge.

'From the *Gazette*,' he explained. 'I understand there've been developments.'

'No need to tell me.'

'Of what nature may I enquire?'

'All depends where you make a start, don't it? First one gets done for.' She paused to let this be absorbed.

'I see,' said Haresnip, though he didn't.

'Well, that puts the cat among the pigeons, as you might say.'

'What cat?'

The woman stared at him, as if doubting whether she'd heard right. 'It weren't no cat it were a dog.'

'You mean?'

But instead of answering she put her fingers to her nose, blew out her cheeks and made a farting noise.

'Do you mean. . . ?'

'Vomiting, that's what some was driven to. What done it? You better ask them what knows.'

'And who would they be?'

'Now you're askin'.'

'That's right,' Haresnip said encouragingly.

'Well there's some what lives like gypsies, wouldn't you say?'

Haresnip began to guess. 'You mean in a caravan?'

Now she was standing sideways to him, looking out over the old lady's wood.

'The problem is . . .'

'No, you can't go that way.' She jerked her head towards the church. 'That be through her garden. You best try down there,' she said, nodding in the opposite direction. 'Down Chestnut Avenue that is – though there b'ain't bin no chestnuts, long as I remembers, and halfway down, well, not quite, if you see what I mean, there be a kind of what d'yer call it, not a stile like because the youth club broke that down, that is when we had a youth club, and some says we should be havin' one again, but not with this 'ere reverend – the Reverend Turkey Stuffing, I calls him, his name being Sage, though not to his face for sure.'

'The problem is,' Haresnip said, 'I went there before and nearly got eaten by an angry dog.' Not to mention a large young woman, he was about to add.

'That one won't do no eating no more,' she said. 'Seeing he's bin eaten hisself in a manner of speaking.'

'Can't pretend I'm sorry.'

'. . . And if you wanter know how that come about, well, how would I know? 'Cos there's bin goings on and no mistake since you was last visiting, and that one's got his comeuppance too and no mistake.'

Now thoroughly confused, Haresnip set off down Chestnut Avenue, clambered over the wrecked stile, and reached Lorna's stream some distance higher than before. Here the drought had reduced it to a trickle between beds of reed. Following it, he presently found his way blocked by brambles, boldly set out to cross and had successfully reached the far bank where he was emptying sludge from a shoe when he realized he was in the path of a thundering horse. No choice but to stagger back into the boggy rushes which turned out to be laced with stinging nettles. Attempting to keep his shoeless foot out of danger he tumbled sideways onto his knees.

'Didn't you see me coming?' Gertie Jones yelled, as she careered past with drumming hoofs. By the time she came round again, after making the animal jump several horizontal poles it could easily have avoided, he was back on the bank, much stung but at least wearing two shoes again. Now the huge animal skidded to a halt and its rider extracted from the pocket of a commando-style jacket a pair of glasses, rimmed in sky blue plastic.

'You all right?' she shouted at him.

'I suppose so.'

'Trouble is, he thinks this meadow is his. Reckon he took you for some kind of a water monster.'

'I've been called many things.' Haresnip began.

'You lost your way? Can I help?'

'Actually, yes. I gather something else has happened down here. Did you by any chance. . . ?'

'See anything? No. Smell it? You're telling me. Two fields away we were.' Herself and the horse, she meant. Now she put the animal into an instant gallop. 'Maybe they can explain,' she yelled back, pointing in the general direction of the wood.

Haresnip shrugged his shoulders, continued along the meadow bank, presently reached a bridge and saw beyond it the caravan. Now that every tree and shrub was in full leaf it looked even less distinguishable from them. Its sagging door was shut and bleached curtains drawn. Cautiously he approached, peered round one end, and saw rags, presumably once clothes, drying on bramble bushes, sooty saucepans upside down on a patch of grass, and a small duckling. He turned back – and was instantly facing a short, remarkably broad girl, presumably the one who'd shouted at him from the caravan's window. Out in the open, she suggested a female heavyweight.

'What do *you* want?'

'Oh hallo, oh nothing, well, in fact I was wondering if you could help.' No reply, Haresnip blundered on, 'I gather there was a bonfire down here. A dog . . '

'What's that to do with you?'

'Well, in a sense, it could be. You may think it absurd but our readers love animal stories, the more tragic the better. We ran the tale of the starving gerbils of The Limes, Mill Lane, for six weeks. I once did a count. All but one of the last eighteen issues had a 'pet' story on the front page. And the eighteenth had one about our MP, which you may think much the same.'

The girl didn't laugh. The longer she stared at him the more clearly she seemed to be telling him to clear off.

Uncertain what to do next, Haresnip was surprised to see the same woman in flower-print dress bearing down on him from above, clutching at successive tree trunks to prevent herself falling.

'I thought you said that was private?' he called to her.

'For furriners,' she said, arriving close to him but panting. 'Well now' – noticing his soaked trouser legs – 'you bin in the wars?'

'After a fashion.'

'And what are they telling?'

'To be honest, not a lot.'

'Well wouldn't you reckon it coincidental like, one dorg getting done then another, just as sudden like?'

'Oh, has there been another?'

'Did I say that? Tell you what, you follow the path' – she

pointed downstream – 'and maybe you'll find one as can be more helpful.'

'Who should I ask for?'

'Well, likely you'll not find that one, seeing he'll be away making his pitzi things.' She paused. 'Some says they seen his mother.'

Haresnip climbed through the wood – private or not, he wasn't going near that stream again.

'You just turn left soon as you reach the road,' she yelled after him, 'and look for the only big one, modern like – b'ain't more than two or three that way.'

Soon he was crossing a lawn where an ancient lady perched on a shooting stick under a sun shade watched him the whole way but said not a word. Christ, what a spooky place! He reached the road again and set off towards the village's outskirts. As he went he fingered his neck to test for swellings. One bite was so painful it might have been a wasp sting. True, he remembered being stung by a wasp when a little boy on the beach at Southsea and he'd survived that, but wasn't it the second that usually proved fatal. Wasps – or was it bees? – left their stings behind them and as a result they died – serve them right – but couldn't these fester? And what happened if they got mixed up with whatever nettles had, producing a cocktail of poisons which might even now be surging about inside him?

These worrying thoughts so occupied him that before he expected it he found himself close to tall iron railings, these surrounding the only large house he'd passed. Still not sure, he was reaching a hand towards the railings for support when a glistening scarlet car slithered to a halt behind him and a dark man two-thirds normal height jumped out and began to yell at him. To make sure he was being heard he did this with his face about six inches from Haresnip's – a sure sign of excess testosterone, Haresnip had read.

Among a torrent of abuse Haresnip thought he heard 'criminal damage' several times. Detaching himself from the railings – carefully, in case he was accused of injuring them – he moved a fraction sideways to be out of the path of the man's spittle and explained that he was from the local press. Was it true that the gentleman had recently lost his dog?

A silence followed, in such contrast to the earlier yells that Haresnip thought a more violent eruption might be coming. 'Perhaps you can help me,' he said, and suffered a spasm in his left armpit where he knew his lymphatic glands came closest to the surface.

'So that's who you are,' the man said, with frightening quietness, through what Haresnip would have described in print as 'clenched teeth'. 'I'll tell you something you can put in your rotten paper. Where are those other two mopheads?'

'Mopheads?'

'Weren't there three of them playing in their sand pit?'

Of course, the drowned young man had had assistants - whom everyone seemed to have forgotten.

'Weren't they screaming at each other all evening?'

'Were they? When? On the night of the accident? Did you hear them?'

'Peace and love, that's their act. Don't you believe it. They're as peaceful as a nest of hornets.'

Oh shit, could it have been a hornet bite?

'I'll tell you someone else you can bother instead of terrifying people's invalid mothers with your banging and shouting—'

'I never—'

'Next house on the right.'

'With the turret?'

'Any moment now that gentleman won't know what hit him. He'll be in court, charged with assault.'

'Will he? Assaulting your dog?'

'You better ask him that.'

The conversation was apparently over because the man began to unchain his gates.

'Thank you for your help,' Haresnip said.

He was ten yards away and still shivering when the man yelled after him, 'I know your editor,' so loudly that Haresnip found his head jerked round to make sure he wasn't being followed.

No answer to his knocking, Haresnip explored a side path, reached a walled garden, and there she was, laid out on a patch of grass, totally – yes, Haresnip had to rub his eyes and blink several times – undeniably, completely naked. In the brilliant sunlight she seemed to shimmer, as though coated in glittering oil.

'Hallo,' he began – needed to say it twice because the first time it became a croak.

'Hallo you.' Apparently quite unembarrassed, she rolled on to an elbow and took off the one thing she was wearing – large round sunglasses.

'Actually, I came to speak to your father.'

She laughed loudly. 'You make a joke.' She had a foreign accent, too! Any moment and Haresnip would have a mishap in his underpants. She patted the grass. 'Is nice here. You explain me.'

Haresnip approached, but three feet away his courage failed and he sat on the lawn. 'Is he at home?'

'Be brave boy.' She stroked the grass right alongside one naked buttock. Cautiously he edged his own a couple of feet closer.

'The man who brought you to that funeral.'

This was even funnier. 'He is not my father.'

'Really.'

'He is my good friend.'

'I see. Well, I came to speak to him.'

'Oh,' she said, stopped laughing and gazed into the valley. Pouting, Haresnip felt sure – he'd often wondered what that word meant.

'Has gone away,' she said.

'Far away?'

'Hospital.'

'Oh dear. Is he ill?'

'Perhaps.'

'You mean they haven't diagnosed. . . ?'

'Oh yes, they know. He has hurt his onions. You not understand? He has, how you say, balls ache.'

Now she cocked up her knees, folded her arms round them, laid her head sideways on top and grinned at him. 'Shall we not talk of him?'

'As you like,' Haresnip said. But, deprived of this subject, he was lost for another. Nor did she help, but only kept her head there on one side, grinning at him.

'Well I suppose—' he began.

'First time I see you,' she interrupted, 'I think, what a lovely boy.'

Could he be hearing correctly? The hair stylist to whom Haresnip was engaged had never mentioned it. When in a mood she would sometimes call him blue beard, but in no very affectionate way.

'Oh you English, you are so funny. So randy – is that what you say?'

'It could be.'

'So stiff on top, and underground – well, so stiff also.'

145

Haresnip laughed.

'Do I make joke?'

Unbelievably, she was reaching a nut-brown hand towards him. Haresnip bent forward and grabbed it. Soon he was sitting cosily side by side with her. Then he was stroking her soft, but well-oiled, arm, her thigh . . . Suddenly, with surprising strength she pushed him on to his back, knelt and began to do amazing things to his trousers. 'I show you.'

So it came about very soon afterwards, that Keith Haresnip was also without his clothes. And a moment later that he had mounted Irma Svenson, third cousin of a baron, in the way four-footed animals do it – and the Japanese, he'd been told.

'Is nice this way?' she said, twisting her head to grin up at him.

'Oh yes, oh yes,' Haresnip cried out. And I don't even know her name.

The office, foul with the sports editor's cigarette smoke, swam around him. Spasmodically he was able to type:

Accusation and counter accusation are spreading like wildfire throughout a doomed village not seven miles from this office. Only a few days after the tragic death of the son of Council Chairman, Sir Rupert Brandish, a pedigree Alsatian belonging to bakery entrepreneur, Mr Joseph Cuff, has been brutally murdered. Now, deep in a woodland glade, Truffle, once the adored pet of Sir Rupert's deceased son, has also died a mysterious death. Many inhabitants of the village, already threatened by a major road building project, are demanding an urgent enquiry before more of their beloved pets go to meet their Maker.

It was all there, Haresnip knew, if only, when he was in full flow, he didn't forget what he was typing and find himself back on that sun-drenched lawn – or in that seven-foot bath, set in polished mahogany, where she had pushed his head under six inches of scented foam before sploshing in with him, or in that four-poster, the bed's posts also of mahogany, where she'd discovered – and anointed – his wounds, and he had loved her twice more.

'What's this about a dog?' the editor enquired. The typed copy lay before him.

'Two dogs,' Haresnip said hopefully.

'Name of first dog?'

'Oh, I forgot.'

The editor shook his head sadly. 'There's such a thing as improvization, young man. Photo?'

'They say it was blown to pieces.'

'Surely someone has a mug shot. I presume it was also much loved.'

'I suppose so,' Haresnip said miserably.

'You suppose! Did you by any chance make enquiries?'

'Neither owner was exactly friendly.'

The editor meditated. He enjoyed this phase of the interview, knowing that it would lead to an inspired headline of his own. He also realized it was past six and as soon as the boy left he could get the bottle of Teachers from his bottom drawer.

'Leave it to me,' he said, and accidentally rewarded Haresnip with a smile.

Sure enough, the dog – described as a mastiff named Rex – got the headline and the bulk of the story. The editor, however, because he was lazy, used Haresnip's account of village suspicions to fill the column and it was these which were of most interest to those in the village since they

THOMAS HINDE

seemed to confirm their suspicions.

Over the tree-fringed horizon the sun set among feathery pink clouds in an orange tinted sky. Not a breath of wind. From far away in various directions engines could be faintly heard. Miles down the valley there were occasional hoots and chuffs where the members of the local railway society were playing at puffer trains with a real engine, but these, too, seemed to Gertie Jones to be in another world. She was standing in Geoff Riddle's farmyard where she had come to give Tobias his good-night concentrates and a nuzzle.

Geoff himself was somewhere across the yard, but he was hard to pick out in the dusk. That could be him in the barn doorway behind the shrunken haystack, or it could be his idiot donkey. Though not sentimental, it seemed to Gertie that she and Geoff – and Tobias, even perhaps the donkey – were sharing a moment of evening peace which was what this village was all about, the sort of peace which would soon be gone.

It was indeed Geoff in the barn doorway, but he was less at peace. Quarter of an hour earlier two police cars had sped up the lane beside which the farm stood. Anyone watching Geoff would then have seen him step quickly into cover, his wonky eyes jumping left and right in alarm. Would they come back? If they did, Geoff was afraid he knew why, knew that he should never have taken to keeping his old musket out here. He'd only done it for convenience. Otherwise, by the time he fetched it every pigeon would be halfway across the county.

On the day of the dog's assassination, as soon as he'd heard the shots he'd come clambering up from the twenty-acre at the valley bottom and when he'd reached the barn there it was, exactly where he usually kept it, behind the ancient mangle shredder, the box of cartridges hidden

148

between two sacks of feed. What he'd heard could have been a car back-firing, he reassured himself. Anyway his friend Ralph wouldn't have played him such a dirty trick, however much trouble he was in. As for the shots, wasn't one shot just like another? If only he didn't seem to remember that the barrels had seemed to be warm when he touched them.

CHAPTER TEN

THE MINISTER

FRED Fisher also slept uneasily. He was worried about tomorrow. Tomorrow the minister was coming.

During the afternoon Sir Rupert Brandish had phoned. 'We're bringing forward arrangements by a couple of hours.'

'To nine o'clock?'

'Correct.'

'I see. May we ask why?'

'Ask the minister. Another engagement, presumably.'

'Of greater importance.'

'More than likely.'

'Should I make an announcement?'

'I don't think the minister would want that.'

'But if he wants to meet local people.'

'*If* he wants,' Sir Rupert said, and rang off.

Fred Fisher turned it over and over in his mind. People were to be cheated, and he could imagine how he would feel if this were done to him. Furthermore it might later be discovered that he'd known of the time change and this would make him unpopular. Above all he liked to be popular with everyone and annoyingly this included Sir Rupert. For months he'd been aware that his role as the leader of opposition to the Road Plan was not pleasing the council, and Sir Rupert *was* the council.

Around two in the morning Frederick realized that he was wider awake than he'd been at midnight. It was then that an unexpected thing happened. Suddenly he urgently desired his wife, Wendy, snoring softly two feet away from him. Fred was wearing no pyjamas – he never did – so that wasn't a problem, and Wendy always wore a bell-shaped nightdress – her quick release parachute, they used playfully to describe it. In those days there would often be no time even for a quick release and, being a short man, he would sometimes end up inside it, with many giggles and shrieks. More recently he'd felt that this garment and the way he ignored its opportunities constituted a reproach. To be honest with himself, which in flashes he attempted, he was also missing Virginia. Tonight in his urgency the nightdress ended up over her head. Gently escaping from it afterwards to kiss her, he sensed that she was only now waking up.

Rolling away, still panting slightly, he felt her turn towards him and put her arms round him. Dear old Wendy, Fred thought, as he allowed himself to be hugged. For several minutes he felt at peace. Worry returned, not only about tomorrow but about the possibility that he'd idiotically risked engendering yet another offspring. Seven o'clock, wearing a paisley pattern silk dressing-gown, he crunched, though hardly tasted, his bran flakes. Decision time was coming closer, and he would probably have continued to fail to decide if Admiral Hawker, his sleep pattern permanently affected by the keeping of the middle watch, had not phoned him at 7.10 a.m.

'That you, Fisher? On parade at ten forty-five – those the orders?'

'Well actually—'

'What's that?'

'In fact—'

'Spit it out, man.'

Jack Hawker reported the news to his wife.

'Our young friend wasn't going to tell us. I soon winkled it out of him.'

'Serve him right,' Anne Hawker said.

'Tight,' said the admiral. 'At seven in the morning. What I've suspected all along.'

Anne Hawker made phone calls and presently set out to call on those who hadn't answered. The summer held; the temperature had barely fallen overnight and already the sun was raising wisps of steam from dew-damp grass. Lady Hawker perspired, and swore, especially when she needed to descend through Lorna Furnival's wood to thump on the rotting door of her daughter's hide-out. Though she more or less hid it from herself, Anne Hawker sympathized with Briony. Long ago when she used to run the village Brownies, she herself had been in love with little freckle-faced patrol leader, Zoe Manifold. She'd never, of course, told Jack.

'It's your mother,' she shouted.

'Mummee!' Briony called in exasperation from inside.

Lady Hawker explained.

'Mummee, go away.'

All the same, five minutes later Briony released Sandra from the hug in which she'd held her most of the night and soon afterwards the two of them, Sandra with baby Foxglove in her scarlet kangaroo pouch, emerged from

Lorna Furnival's front gate.

Soon other people were standing at their gates. The presentation of a petition with fifty-three signatures collected by Anne Hawker was the plan, but already there were signs of exasperation at the weakness of this gesture. Sam Langridge had discovered the seven-foot ramrod with moth-eaten mophead which he'd once used to clear blockages in the sewage system in the valley, and stood holding it like a halberd at the entrance to Chestnut Lane. Alongside the village street the Prone boys and girls could occasionally be glimpsed as Justin led them skirmishing among the bushes. Even landlord Wilf Wodge, rarely seen before 11.00 a.m., had been infected by the general excitement and stood with his friend Mr Mullins outside Evan Mullins's failed village shop, remembering occasionally the shaking he'd given his wife Joan for damaging a beer pump, both of them ready to jeer at the shambles they expected. Outside the church Geoff Riddle sat on his tractor, a cabinless Fordson, circa 1950, revving its engine every half-minute to prevent it stalling. A dozen tombstones away, Gertie Jones sat astride Tobias. Tobias was angry too, whisked his tail and bit at his sides where horseflies had bitten him. Across her knees Gertie held a huntsman's crop with a six-foot lash, and in each side pocket of her camouflage jacket an egg, stolen from Geoff's hen house – the converted body of a Ford Transit van.

A short way to the west, Mr Taylor's garden was a curious contrast to other village gardens, mostly in what Polly Langridge called their summer glory. A single Chilean potato tree flourished in one roadside corner but seemed in the nature of a diversion from the slope which rose above and had become as grassy as a meadow. In front of the trench in which Mr Taylor was still sometimes seen at work from the waist up he and Mrs Volga now sat on camp stools. She wore a large straw hat of Mexican peasant style, he a small white sun hat of the sort children once wore on the beach, since then adopted by Australian cricketers afraid of melanoma. Mrs Volga had had a strange dream. She had been a little girl again and Mr Taylor was holding a red watering-can. She was lying naked on her back and he was watering her between the legs. He was doing it so gently, all the time asking whether it hurt.

'Is he not wonderful?' she called to Lorna Furnival, making her way cautiously past with her stick. 'Is he not genius? In my country he would be heaped up with medals.'

Lorna Furnival scowled. She hadn't intended to come. All her life she had resisted doing things other people did. 'What's it to do with me?' she had growled, when Anne Hawker phoned, and poured herself half a tumbler of Madeira. But here she was, in pain, and expecting the worst.

The crowd in and around the churchyard had swelled to thirty or forty people many of whom rarely took part in village affairs apart from grumbling to each other at the school gate. Some had brought children in prams to enjoy this free entertainment, others their dogs, one a Siamese cat in a cat harness.

Meanwhile, propped outside Miss Wiggum's cottage was the Revd Charlie Sage's bicycle. He'd risen early to allow time for this visit. As a school governor it was his duty to investigate rumours about the headmistress. She'd been seen, it was said, at work in her school office in the small hours of the morning, wearing a garment which looked like a nightdress. By day the school remained closed.

No answer at the front or back doors, he tiptoed down the garden path to peep through a window. And there she was, still in that ambiguous dress, sitting upright at her kitchen table facing a boiled egg.

He returned to the back door and found that it was unlocked.

'Glad to see you so much better.'

She stared at him as if she couldn't believe what she was hearing, then plunged her spoon into the egg in a worryingly fierce way and carried a mouthful which dripped yolk on its way to her mouth. Earlier spoonfuls had also dripped, Charlie Sage saw from a trail across the tablecloth.

'I've heard . . . people have been telling me you've not been well.'

When speaking to others Charlie Sage often stood with one foot forward and one back, alternately putting his weight on each as if undecided about whether to attack or bolt.

'To be frank, they say you've been overworking.'

Miss Wiggum couldn't answer because of egg.

'If there's one thing we all need it's a good night's sleep. Seven and a half hours, my old dad used to say, but for me, nothing less than eight fits the bill. Otherwise my sermons become all higgledy piggledy,' he joked, and paused for a laugh, but doubted if she was listening. She had a pen in her hand, and was writing on a piece of paper. When she'd finished she pushed it away as if telling him to read it if he was interested.

He stepped close and read: PERSECUTION.

'I see, ah yes, I see.'

Charlie Sage did not see. Persecution of whom, by whom?

'You mean?' Surely someone in a normal state of mind would have explained, but Miss Wiggum didn't.

'Well, must be getting along. If there's a problem . . .' He struggled for words to explain how willing he was to help, how he was always hoping they would come to ask for it instead of giving him the feeling that he was forcing it on them when they would have preferred to be left in peace. 'If you ever want . . . day or night . . .' But Miss Wiggum was concentrating on her breakfast.

Out in the road he met more villagers moving towards the churchyard as he cycled in the direction of the village's public phone box. Things were worse than he'd expected. Would Dr Sweet still be at home or should he dial 999?

Missing so far from those assembling were Michael Ranch and Mrs Shirley Prone. As the summer baked and shimmered, Michael Ranch's visits to his case at 2 Keats Villas had become weekly, then twice weekly, then daily. Squeezing her bony wrist with his long pale fingers, his mind would be filled with pity. Also with rationalizations. Affection was what she needed, not sedatives and final demands for overdue rent. Wasn't it his duty to provide this? Defiantly he would tell them so if he was ever discovered. At the same time the possibility that he would be *discovered*, disgraced and dismissed, caused him a certain masochistic longing. She was to blame, he told himself, for being so brave, his mind then slithering sideways to his wife, Virginia, who was equally to blame because of her blatant unfaithfulness which he'd tolerated far too long. All that weeping, combined with her rejection of his therapeutic advances.

Meanwhile Frederick Fisher had stationed himself at the point where the road rose towards the village, beside the neighbourhood watch sign. More dignified, perhaps, to have waited by the lych gate where he would have been introduced by Sir Rupert to the minister. 'Kind of you indeed, sir, to spare the time,' he'd begin – or might that sound sarcastic? Finally he'd decided that it was essential to explain in advance to Sir Prosper that it had not been possible to keep secret the minister's changed schedule. The minister might even be grateful for a warning of trouble ahead. 'I thought it wise, sir, to alert you, sir.' 'You did right, Fisher . . .' 'Oh shite' – in his distress this long forgotten word emerged as, round the bend a shiny black car appeared, its engine so soft that he saw it before he heard it, and with a disdainful toot swept past him. He was trotting in pursuit when two more cars, as shiny black but not quite so long, forced him to stumble on to the grass verge while they also swept past.

The minister's formal welcome, supposing someone had had the enterprise to give him one in his own absence, must have been delivered long ago by the time Fred, drenched with sweat and swearing to himself, arrived at the church. The three cars each with its smoking driver, were parked in the road, but the official party was nowhere to be seen. In what direction should he go? Horse droppings in the road . . . Gertie Jones's Tobias no doubt, and they would have come from its rear end, of course, but which way had the stupid animal been pointing? Paraffin fumes – that was better. Now from the direction of open country he thought he could hear the clanking noise of Geoff Riddle's tractor, suggesting as always that the machine was disintegrating.

If he was right many of the crowd should have been looking in the direction which the official party had taken. Instead, as far as he could see through eyes misted with sweat, many seemed to stare at *him*. It was as if his distress was even more obvious than he'd realized, so obvious that they could hardly believe what they were seeing. Some seemed to be horribly laughing. Now one was approaching him, bending – oh dear, Polly Langridge – doing something to his trousers. His instinct was to swat her away; he even had a momentary fantasy that she was trying to unzip them, but no, she was brushing at them as if to remove dirt. Of course, he remembered that, in his haste, he'd stumbled and no doubt greened the knees of his light-weight beige suit specially bought for this occasion. His gratitude to Polly for her kindness brought him close to tears, though he didn't dare thank her for fear they would trickle out, could only smile, nod and set off in the direction of that prehistoric tractor.

At last he saw them, far down the lane, opposite Geoff Riddle's farmyard, and reduced his pace from a shambling jog to a rapid walk. Soon he started to identify them. Central were three grey-suited figures in line abreast: the minister and Sir Rupert, of course, the third, from his expansive arm-waving seemed probably to be the landscape architect. Behind followed some girls with notepads – private secretaries? – and two wide-shouldered men in ill-fitting suits – detectives? Like outriders, farmer Riddle drove his machine ahead and Gertie Jones walked her horse behind. The whole party seemed to be going further into the country so he would either have to hurry to overtake them, or wait for them to come back. But a moment later he saw that he'd been wrong and they were already coming towards him. Now he slowed his walk and prepared to meet them, face to face.

Coming towards him so fast now that he felt different alarm. Were they so busy talking to each other that they were going to march past him without noticing him, let alone stopping? Closer and closer they came, two of them listening, the architect waving towards woods and fields a thousand years old, conjuring up visions of endless suburbia, that it was only at the last moment that Fred had a clever idea: a dying aunt. Even so it needed courage to stand fully in their path.

'Good morning,' he called loudly. This more or less stopped them. 'Unfortunately my aunt has suffered a stroke . . .' It was hopelessly wrong. He hadn't even explained who he was.

Sir Rupert was not helpful, stopped and stared at Fred as if intentionally drawing attention to this curious person's greened knees, and his still odder remark.

'Ah, yes, Minister, this is . . .' He hesitated, pretending to have forgotten the name – our local PC chairman, Mr . . . Who has taken a tumble I see.'

It was now that Frederick Fisher knew that he would never forgive Sir Rupert Brandish. For a second his mind seemed to turn black with anger. Stepping rudely across the others he held out his hand to the minister. 'Frederick Fisher's the name.'

In automatic response the minister's hand jerked forward. It was so unpleasantly soft and damp that Fred, increasingly bold, pulled his own away and turned to the architect. 'Who are *you*?' he asked.

'Sir Wilfred, this is our Mr Fisher, leader of local opinion,' Sir Rupert explained. 'His aunt—'

'What are we waiting for?' Fred interrupted, and placed himself fourth in the line.

So they progressed back towards the church, Fred on the left flank able several times to block Sir Wilfred's expansive gestures. When they came close to the first villagers, however, he detached himself to stand among them.

'Didn't want to dirt their shoes, did they?' Polly Langridge called loudly.

'Forgot their galoshes,' Sam, her husband, called, his sewage ramrod now shouldered like a rifle.

159

As the hostile murmuring became general, Fred was inspired. 'NIMBY,' he shouted. 'NIMBY NIMBY NIMBY.' Though most had forgotten what this meant, it sounded rude and several began to shout with him, creating enough of a disturbance to encourage a couple of ill-dressed fellows with cameras, who might be the national press, to start dodging about ahead of the official party and creating flashes.

Others had also arrived. Mr Taylor and Mrs Russia, carrying their camping stools; Jack and Anne Hawker, she with the petition; Geoff Riddle on his belching machine; Ralph Gamble, his doggy jowls today a mauve background to their fine pink veins, standing close to Irma Svenson who seemed to be supporting him; Keith Haresnip who had come early in the hope of – he didn't quite know what – only to see this disappointing development; Ernest Boon, who kept edging close to Lorna Furnival. When at last he arrived alongside her he told her in a whisper, 'She's back.'

'Speak up.'

'My wife. Tiffany.'

'From New Zealand?'

'Well, in point of fact—'

Now Lorna saw her, peering over the churchyard wall, staring fiercely at her husband.

'Good God,' Lorna said. But she had another matter to attend to, was advancing on the largest of those black cars, calling to its driver, 'You're parked on my grass', and when he didn't seem to hear, banging on his windscreen with her stick.

The driver rolled down his window an inch and tossed his butt at her feet. 'Sorry, ma'am,' he said, with exaggerated subservience and started his engine. He meant perhaps to repark near the school, but to get there he needed to pass the church and a crowd now blocked his way. Though some villagers moved aside, Mrs Volga and Mr Taylor remained sitting on their stools, she gripping his wrist to hold him down. As a result the car was forced to halt directly in front of a wooden platform which had been erected against the churchyard's wall for the minister to mount when he spoke. For some minutes it seemed that this might not happen. He, Sir Rupert and Sir Wilfred were quite rudely jostled as they edged their way towards its steps.

Anne Hawker followed them, at the same time opening the wooden clappers of her cloth bag to extract the petition. 'Here you are,' she shouted, holding it out to the minister.

'Thank you, thank you,' he said, but the way he stared at it suggested that he hadn't been warned about this part of the programme. He was tall, with, perched between his shoulders, a baby face, every feature of which – eyes, cheeks, nose, lips – bulged as if it had once been given a heavy blow on top and things below forced outwards.

'Petition,' Sir Rupert hissed at him.

'Indeed, indeed,' the minister said. 'Very pleased. Glad you realize we are a listening government. Committed to taking account of all shades of local opinion,' then stopped himself from further plundering his prepared address.

'How the devil will you do that?' Anne Hawker asked, still halfway up the steps.

'No shade?' the admiral said, supporting his wife from a lower step. 'Wasn't the fellow ever in the tropics?'

Sir Rupert Brandish introduced the minister. 'We are privileged to have with us today—'

'Oh yeah!' Sam Langridge called.

'Despite his heavy schedule—'

Now there was ironic laughter. Somewhat impatiently the minister waited for Sir Rupert, who was no orator, to finish. The minister believed he knew better how to capture an audience's sympathy. At last he was allowed to draw his speech from his pocket and begin softly, 'I well understand your concern—'

'Louder,' Gertie Jones yelled.

'I can well understand,' the minister read more loudly.

'Can't hear you,' Gertie Jones yelled.

No longer curling his bulbous lips into an endearing smile, the minister tried once more.

Gertie yelled again. Now others joined her. 'We can't hear you,' they chanted.

'Who is she?' Sir Rupert asked, red in the face with fury, but found no one except Sir Wilfred to ask.

'Regrettable,' Sir Wilfred murmured.

Turning to the crowd, Sir Rupert shouted, 'You're not doing your cause any good.'

'Not doing our cause no good,' some chanted.

'Silly old geezer,' Gertie Jones cried.

'Get her away,' Sir Rupert shouted.

This was a mistake. When the two moustached detectives tried to grip the horse's bridle, Gertie released her huntsman's whip, at the same time giving Tobias, already in a foul mood, a kick in the ribs and jerk in the mouth which caused him to rise on to his hind legs and strike out with his front feet. The two detectives fled, one tripping on to his knees, the other reaching with his right hand inside the left flap of his jacket, as if for a shoulder holster. At the same time Gertie made no effort to prevent Tobias kicking with his hind legs and giving the glossy black wing of the blocked limousine a blow which so frightened him he bolted through the crowd and set off up the village street at a gallop. Calm returned temporarily and the minister took the opportunity to resume his speech.

'As you know, or, may I suggest, *should* know, this government is committed to returning power to the people. Top of our agenda is the enhancing of the responsibilities of local government. I won't pretend that this will always result in decisions pleasing to everyone, but you will all' – he paused to emphasize his point – 'every one of you have the comfort of knowing that such decisions have been reached in a democratic manner . . .'

'Comfort, my arse,' said Sam Langridge.

'Blithering old faggot,' Polly Langridge said.

The longer the minister continued the more he lost any sympathy they might have felt for him, because of his silly face. Not that his words affected Admiral Jack Hawker one way or another. Sandwiched in the narrow corridor between the minister's car and the platform, he had begun to use his stick to bang on its planks. 'Did you mention the tropics?' he called up.

'The minister is speaking,' Sir Rupert shouted at him.

'And a lot of nonsense, too.'

'Be quiet, whoever you are.'

It was the excuse Briony had waited for. 'He's my father,' she shouted and, abandoning Sandra and child, took hold of the ends of the platform's planks which she began to bang up and down. Being strong she lifted them each time perhaps six inches into the air before letting them fall back with a crash.

'Whoops,' the architect, Sir Wilfred, said, as the three of them staggered about, barging each other as they made for the steps. Before they could reach them, however, these – never firmly attached – toppled on to their side. Left with no other escape they staggered, arms waving, to the steadier end of the platform and, in turn, jumped, two landing on their knees, the minister in the arms of Mrs Volga. It was her opportunity to deliver her message into an important ear.

'You kill him,' she shouted, 'with thousands of little cuttings.'

She'd to shout for there was now general tumult, to which the sound of Tobias returning, still at a gallop added excitement. There were other noises, at first unexplained: a succession of echoing bangs. Things were falling on to the roof of the car and indiscriminately everywhere else. The whole assembly was now apparently under bombardment from a shower of unripe, quite heavy apples. Here and there the Prone boys and girls could be seen crouched with their supplies of fruit behind tombstones. Among them Tiffany Boon had mounted the stone lid of an eighteenth-century box tomb. 'Injured this way,' she shouted. Here and there photographers hopped, flashed and occasionally shouted if someone got in their way. There was almost too much to please them; late that night, in his darkroom, one ginger-haired young man was rewarded with a shot of the minister clasped in Mrs Volga's arms.

It was, in fact, Tobias who was destroying Mr Taylor's life work. Scared by encountering a wobbling black-clothed cyclist – the Revd Charlie Sage – he'd jumped Mr Taylor's hedge at one end and galloped his garden's length including an accidental tumble into his trench. Blowing steam and foam, barely under Gertie's control, he now careered towards the mêlée in front of the church. 'Stand back,' Gertie screamed, but already he was among them, then through them and clattering away into the countryside. Whether, however, it was Tobias's hooves which did the damage to Mr Taylor's garden, or someone else had already done most of it with a bill hook was to be much discussed.

Long before the clatter had faded, a more alarming noise could he heard approaching from the other direction: police sirens. Later it was presumed that one of the detectives had called for them on his pocket radio. They took longer to arrive than they might have done, delayed by Dr Sweet's car, meandering uphill in the middle of the road. Dr Sweet was wondering whether he had remembered to bring with him his bag of potions, as he liked to call his medicine chest. Why was everyone always in such a hurry, he thought, refusing to let him pass? As if they couldn't wait to be dead.

Shouts, howls, cheers and the sound of those police sirens came faintly up the hill to Keats Villas and in through the rarely opened windows of Number 2's front room. Here Shirley Prone lay on her back on the sofa with Michael Ranch's pale hand inside her T-shirt. He had fought – how he'd fought – against his desire. But for those noises from the village below he might have won. The sense they gave him of a wild world in which he might just as well take part, had finally defeated his good intentions, not to mention his reputation as a caring welfare officer.

'Well I never!' Shirley Prone had said, when he forced her flat, removed her slippers, unzipped her jeans and lifted her buttocks to help him remove them.

Michael Ranch was in no mood to be put off by her sarcasm. His member throbbed, and he was forcing it through her carrot coloured bush when he heard running steps. Closer and closer they came until, with a crash, some-one seemed to throw himself against the door which Shirley had wisely locked.

'Mum, Mum, they got him.'

Shirley Prone climbed back into her jeans, pushed her feet into her down-trodden slippers and stood inside her door.

'Who's there?'

'It's me, Mum, Winston and 'oward.'

'Well you just stop frigging around and explain yerself.'

165

'It's Justin, Mum. They took him away. The law.'

'What was he doing.'

'He weren't doin nothin, Mum.'

Shirley Prone opened the door but stayed in the doorway. 'Don't you give me that,' she said savagely.

'Well, nothing criminal like. He rund out of apples, see.'

'Well?'

'So he has this spiky thing. It don't do no harm. You just pokes wiv it and the air comes out so it goes flat. They got him when he done just the one.'

'Where is he now?'

'Took 'im away, they did.'

Michael Ranch, fully clothed, now arrived. 'Hallo, Winston.'

' 'allo, Mr Ranch.'

'Your brother's been arrested?'

'S'right.'

A pause while Michael Ranch considered his duty.

' 'E din go quiet, Mr Ranch,' Winston Prone said, detecting sympathy. 'You oughter see 'em, all puffin and pantin' in their posh clothes, tryin' to get 'im in.'

'I shall deal with this,' Michael Ranch said.

'You fucking won't,' Mrs Prone said. 'Whose kids do you think they are?'

CHAPTER ELEVEN

MOPPING UP

FRED Fisher drove Mrs Prone to the police station where he began an unsatisfactory discussion with the duty officer about police rights to arrest and detain juveniles. At no special point Shirley Prone started to scream. She didn't use words but a continuous, high-pitched squeal, so loud that Fred wanted to block his ears, but didn't because this seemed disloyal.

At his desk in his backroom office the chief inspector listened to the noise for some minutes then gave orders that it must stop. Fred Fisher drove Shirley Prone and Justin back to the village.

'You barmy little twit,' Mrs Prone began the interrogation. She was slightly hoarse.

Justin sulked.

'Tell us what happened,' Fred Fisher encouraged him.

'They 'it me.'

'They did?' Fred and Mrs Prone both became interested. 'Where?'

'All over.'

By good luck as they arrived in the village street Dr Sweet was emerging from Miss Wiggum's cottage, and agreed to carry out an examination. In the Prone front room where Michael Ranch sat uneasily in an armchair, left behind as child minder, the doctor discovered a graze on one of Justin's shins the result of skidding into a tombstone, and a slight reddening of one ear.

'Tell me if any bruises develop,' Dr Sweet said, in the doorway.

'You bet I will,' Shirley Prone said.

Fred drove on to find a turning place. The village seemed strangely quiet. All that remained outside the churchyard wall were the wooden platform with its collapsed steps, a widespread scattering of crushed and uncrushed apples and horse droppings flattened into brown pancakes. He stopped, got out and looked about him. The sun shone, the sky was blue, momentarily the wind stirred the trees then died away. Unsure what he was looking for, he got back in and drove home.

The impression was deceptive. In private various things were happening. Ernest Boon had set off for Meadowsweet more slowly than others had dispersed, glancing back for a last sight of the dissolving gathering, wondering how Tiffany, who had gone ahead, would welcome him. For thirty years he'd made similar guesses, rarely with success. But while in the past he had half looked forward to, even admired the way she could surprise him, he now found the idea annoying. He was no longer looking forward to an explanation of why the escape to New Zealand had been cancelled, suspecting that it had always been an attempt to frighten him. More interestingly, in her absence he had begun to realize that life without Tiffany was agreeably peaceful. He could come indoors without wiping his shoes, dry his hands on the tea towel, sniff when his nose ran.

The sight of her establishing a first aid post on top of an eighteenth-century box tomb had finally shown him his wife the way others must see her, and in consequence the way they must see him. This was not pleasant. The sight of the massive Briony Hawker tilting those dignified gentlemen off their platform had been another eye-opener. In an instant and without the smallest qualification he'd admitted to himself what he'd long half known, that he loved Briony Hawker, passionately, as he had presumably once loved Tiffany – in nurse's uniform, bringing him cups of malted milk while he recovered from a strangulated hernia. Try as he would, he could now only imagine that long ago emotion as if it had been experienced by another person.

Briony's strong, short arms, the way their muscles had stood out as she strained to lift the platform's planks, the way her jaw had set and her short dark hair seemed to rise with the effort – it was absurd of course, at his age, at her age – he thought, as he turned back for a last glance, and bumped into Mrs Volga. The thought of lying half suffocated underneath Briony Hawker, the arrangement he imagined, gave him a distracting erection.

It also brought him out in sweat at the thought of Tiffany noticing, which she surely would, and misinterpreting it. 'Put that thing away, you old goat,' he could hear her saying. And since imagining this, instead of deflating it, made it rise more defiantly, he avoided his front door and went into his back garden to sprinkle anti-cat pepper around his lettuce seedlings.

In his front garden at the other end of the village Sam Langridge had planted his sewage-clearing ramrod, head upwards, where its matted strands gave it the character of an unwashed Rastafarian. He and Polly occasionally opened their front door to admire it.

'That'll show 'em,' Sam said.

'I should hope so,' Polly said.

'What 'appens now?'

'Ask yer grandmother.'

Two hundred yards further down Chestnut Lane, Virginia Ranch sat at her sitting-room writing-table. 'Dear Fred,' she wrote – and again burst into tears. This was as far as she'd got, though she'd been writing to Fred Fisher for several hours and meaning to write to him for three months. It was the glimpse of him between her drawn curtains, wearing that ridiculous, obviously new, tropical-weight suit which had finally told her how he needed her.

As the weeks had passed she'd done her best to believe that he had used her, not loved her. Three months' neglect – she'd forgotten several deliveries of expensive flowers – and then imagining he could drop in for a quick fuck. She'd forced herself to think the nasty word though it made her shudder and had several times caused tears to drip on to her writing paper.

'Dear Mr Fisher. . . .' The things she'd let him do to her, the places he'd inserted that prickly black beard, not to mention his tongue – oh oh! Too horrible. Though even when she'd known that he was self-centred and cruel, remembering these events could still cause her a twinge of excitement, as well as allowing uninvited thoughts to occur to her; for example, if only it had ever happened with Michael.

'Dearest Freddie . . .' she tried again, meaning to be gentler, but still determined. Surely she could ask him to understand that it was friendship she needed more than, or at least as much as, the sort of love he gave her. But now she was distracted by a day dream in which she lay in his arms, sobbing, and he held her tightly while whispering loving words in one ear. She crumpled the sheet of Basildon Bond and dropped it on top of others because she knew that this was the Devil tempting her, because up there, grey bearded and wise but stern, looking down from the ceiling, was a face resembling her grandfather's, waiting to judge her by the path she chose.

Mid-afternoon she heard the turning of Michael's latch key. She knew her duty. As soon as he reached the sitting-room doorway she ran towards him with open arms, head tilted slightly back, determined to ask forgiveness for her wickedness.

Michael Ranch was astonished. As he saw her running at him, his first thought was that she held some sharp weapon and was going to stab him. Somehow – God knows how – she must have guessed about him and Shirley. Taking a quick step back, he raised one knee to protect his private parts. When it seemed that she was going to use her spread arms to seize and perhaps shake him, he lifted his own in further defence. It was only when he realized that she was trying to wrap them round him in some kind of hug that he suspected she'd finally gone mad.

For some seconds Virginia continued to try to enfold him. Only when, instead, he gave her a sharp push in the chest, did she abandon these efforts and step away from him. Suddenly she understood everything. Here, standing in front of her, was her persecutor. It was he, her husband, who, in revenge for her unfaithfulness, had fouled her doorstep. The more she thought about it the more obvious it seemed. All his tenderness while she had been ill had been a mockery, hiding his satisfaction that she was being punished. She opened her mouth and howled. 'Oh God, oh my God.' Because *no one* loved her. Now she ran to the door where her handbag had hung unused for three months. A quick glance into it to make sure that it still held her cheque book, then she opened the front door and set off for her spinster aunt who lived in Harrogate.

Michael stood in the doorway. His mouth opened to call to her, but not calling. Instead he returned to their sitting-room where he stood looking down at those wasted sheets of writing paper. How strange. She was usually so economical. Ah well, her absence might be convenient.

Not for long. Twenty minutes later he was astonished to see her returning down the garden path, heard her use her key in the front door then saw her go straight past the sitting-room doorway upstairs to her bedroom.

Softly he followed and listened at its door. Not a sound.

Inside, out of his keyhole view, she sat on the edge of her bed, golden hair for once slightly awry, a writing pad on her knee. 'Dearest Freddie,' she wrote. How could she possibly let him appear in public so ridiculously dressed?

Behind his milking shed, Geoff Riddle dug into the edge of the black mound he called his midden, which he never liked to mount in case he sank to his waist. Into a two-foot trench he presently laid his hammer-action 12-bore, wrapped in black polythene sheeting. For a moment he stared down at it – with his left eye – wondering whether to change his mind. Gertie rattling horse cubes in a pail to comfort Tobias for an upsetting day, decided him and he began to use his shovel and Wellington boots to bury it.

Gertie Jones was high. After regaining control of Tobias and standing him under a shady oak to finish snorting and scraping, she'd returned to the village and trotted him up and down, in search of someone to congratulate her. She was quietly certain that she and Tobias had been heroic.

Around the churchyard all was deserted, the last official limousine, punctured tyre replaced, but the occupants still not speaking to each other, was disappearing down the hill as she arrived. For five minutes she found no one until, approaching the Secret Gardener's garden, she remembered one of the episodes of Tobias's great ride.

'Sorry about that,' she called cheerily. 'The poor fellow got a bit steamed up. Not his fault.' Only now, peering through her sky-blue framed glasses, did she see that Mrs Volga was also there, in her silly straw hat, and that they were staring at devastation which Tobias alone could surely not have created. Even the Chilean Potato Tree had a snapped branch.

'Golly!'

A third person now appeared: Admiral Pink Gin, as Gertie sometimes called Jack Hawker. When the crowd in front of the churchyard wall had dispersed, Jack Hawker had noticed Mr Taylor and remembered the fight they'd had which still caused his coccyx to ache in wet weather. No time for grudges, leaving his wife he caught up with the chap and held out a wrinkled brown hand. 'Let bygones be bygones,' he ordered. Mr Taylor listened, seemed to wince at this burst of friendliness but said nothing.

'Good grief,' the admiral said as they reached Mr Taylor's garden and he saw the devastation.

'Anything I can do?' Gertie offered.

For several minutes they stood together staring in astonishment, then, as if by mutual consent they seemed to realize that they could do nothing to help and it would be kindest to leave him to recover on his own. Gertie trotted away in one direction and the admiral and Mrs Volga hobbled off in the other.

'He should be famous man,' she called back.

'Someone made a famous mess of his garden,' the admiral said.

'Soon he will have nervous breakdown.'

'Breakdown? Car trouble? Damned unreliable things. Remember when they had a starting handle. At least you knew where you were – or weren't! First we had, a decent old Rover. Anne, she's my wife, broke her wrist cranking it up. Gave her quite a fright.'

'He is being threatened.'

'Threatened? Who by? Not that idiot who'd never heard of the tropics?'

'He is so honest. He has made a statement. He will not withdraw. This car, it almost blows his hat off. It goes seventy, eighty miles an hour.'

'Just what I say. Dangerous things. My wife Anne—'

'He is not like every man. He does not have his prices.'

'Prices?' But the subject was so vast, leading off in so many interesting directions, that the Admiral seemed not to know which to follow. They had anyway reached his doorway.

'Nice talking to you. See what we can do about your poor fellows garden. I'll ask my wife. She has a basket of old seed packets, all muddled up, flowers and vegetables together. I told her that one day she'd be giving me cornflowers for breakfast. She thought that rather a good joke.'

'What have you been up to, boy?' Mrs Irene Cuff screeched from her upstairs bedroom door.

'Nothing, Mumsie,' Joseph Cuff answered from the kitchen.

'What are you doing down there?'

'Nothing, Mumsie.' Now he could hear her shuffling and banging about, periodically giving a barking cough. Didn't she understand that he did it for her?

'What's for supper?'

'I've brought you one of my specials.'
'Huh!' But he could tell that she was interested.
'Mushrooms and mortadella with olives and tomatoes.'
'You know olives don't agree.'
'They're good for you, Mumsie.'
'Nonsense.'
'I'll pick them out.'
Silence.

Quietly Joseph Cuff lifted the sickle from the table and carried it to the garage where he hid it under a pile of folded cardboard boxes. He'd thought of putting it behind the cooker, but you never knew where she might poke about. People had to learn, he told himself, glancing up to see if she was watching from her window. If they wouldn't they had to be taught. What would happen to her if he was arrested and held, let alone put away? It was quite possible, as he'd started to explain to her, but she wouldn't listen.

As for those who brought charges – not to mention those who'd murdered Gideon – Joseph Cuff broke into a sweat of fury. He returned to his sitting-room where Mr and Mrs Solomon, his mother's parents, hung in heavy silver frames over the fireplace, and, sitting down at his desk, re-read with satisfaction letters he'd written to his solicitor, and with fury the man's evasive answers, so infuriating they made his heart race, and decided him to go out into the evening sunlight. There he crunched about on the gravel, now silent and dogless, behind his six-foot iron railings, his hairy fists clenching and unclenching. That fellow would find out some people weren't to be witnessed against.

At about the same time, at the bottom of Lorna Furnival's wood, two police constables were taking Sandra away for questioning. A female colleague followed, carrying Foxglove. They'd tried to take Briony as well, but she was too quick for them, bounding up through the wood at remarkable speed, considering her weight and short legs.

Lorna was sitting in an armchair, reading the sports pages of *The Times*. Far from finding these boring, she was concerned about the new appointments at her club, Newcastle, an interest first cultivated to annoy pretentious aesthetes, now genuine.

'Hallo, what's up?'

'Police,' Briony began, and had to stop, still panting. 'Arresting us.'

'Go upstairs and get under a bed. I haven't seen you.'

Up there Lorna heard the squeal of casters, heavy thumps and a crash – possibly a china chamber pot. She should have warned the clumsy girl.

The police arrived half an hour later. Standing at her front window she saw their car stop outside her gate. They must have left the wood by the bottom path and driven up the lane. When they got out she saw that they were the usual pair. She also saw a policewoman, sitting in their car, holding the child. Sandra sat beside them, staring straight ahead.

Lorna opened her front door and stood in the doorway.

'You again!'

'May we have a word with you, Mrs Furnival?' They were at their most solemn.

'I can't stop you.' But she didn't move.

'Well, it's like this,' – the smaller one shuffled a foot before controlling it – 'we're looking for a young woman. Perhaps you can help us.'

'What makes you think so?'

'We understand she's a tenant of yours.'

'My only tenant you seem to have captured already. What right do you have to arrest her?'

'It's being taken care of.'

'*She*. She has a sex, you know.'

'The other young woman was seen escaping in your direction.'

'Was she? What do you want her for? What do you want either of them for?'

'We've things to talk to that one about.' He jerked his head towards the car.

'Not marijuana again?' Lorna banged the boot scraper with her stick. 'Didn't I tell you I grow the stuff for my personal consumption?'

'Possibly we don't believe you, Mrs Furnival.'

'What are you charging her with?'

'There's no intention of bringing a charge. We need to ask them certain questions.'

'About what?'

'I'm afraid we're not at liberty—'

'Attempted manslaughter perhaps?'

'So you witnessed the incident?'

'What incident?' But she'd made a mistake. 'I was thinking of something sufficiently absurd.'

They waited for more, but Lorna had had enough.

'Sorry, I can't help you.' She started to shut the door.

'Mrs Furnival, hindering the police in making an arrest—'

'Are you threatening me?'

'It's our duty—'

'Duty be blowed.' She was losing her temper – always a mistake. 'Young man, how old are you? All right, you're not at liberty to say. Well, I'm seventy-three.'

Now they were embarrassed.

'So you can threaten till you're purple in the face.'

She shut the door and stood at her front window, watching them from a few feet away. They hesitated, then one

177

seemed to say something to the other and they marched away in file.

Stupid, stupid, she thought, but she was still too angry to be sorry. And too worried about what to do. That unexplained white envelope, pinned to one of her trees at the far side of her lawn, with nothing inside it.

She'd have liked to keep young Briony in her attic, enjoyed the idea of taking her bowls of soup. She moved from room to room, still banging things with her stick, arrived at the sideboard, reached for the brandy bottle, but didn't lift it. 'Briony,' she shouted.

After all it wasn't a problem. As soon as Briony knew they'd taken Sandra she wanted to follow. Perhaps she'd already regretted running away. Together she and Lorna went by taxi to the police station.

They weren't expected, it seemed. The duty officer hunted in his log book, made phone calls, disappeared and reappeared behind his counter where he stood silently, as if waiting for an idea to occur to him.

'What officers were those?' he unexpectedly asked.

'Their names? I've no idea. One was tall and one short.'

Difficult to know whether this helped.

When Briony was eventually led away Lorna demanded to see the chief inspector.

'I'll find out. He's probably busy.'

'I'll wait till he isn't.'

Led in at last, she stood in front of his desk, refusing a seat. He was moustached, with short grey hair. In short sleeves without a jacket he seemed uncomfortable.

'What's all this about?' she asked.

He would have liked to be avuncular, Lorna guessed, if her age hadn't made this difficult.

'Why do you need to bring them here to question them?'

'It sometimes helps.'

'Helps to frighten them.'

'Let's say jogs their memory.'

'Why do they need jogging.'

No answer.

'And Miss Hawker, what reason have you for wanting her?'

'It might be for her own good if she didn't make a habit of tipping cabinet ministers off platforms.'

'Is that the only reason?'

For several seconds he didn't answer. Lorna detected evasion.

'Well?'

'That young person's death – the case has not been closed.'

'Shouldn't it be? Anyway, what had she to do with it?'

The chief inspector didn't answer.

'If you're suggesting what I think you are,' Lorna said, 'it's preposterous.'

He sighed, perhaps with genuine regret. 'Sorry, I can't be more help.'

'You mean you're under pressure?'

Again he remained silent, then, staring her straight in the eyes, said, 'Certainly not, Mrs Furnival.' He couldn't have told her more clearly not to believe him. Nor was it difficult to guess who was applyng the pressure.

Lorna grunted.

She needn't wait, he told her. When they'd been questioned they would be delivered home, if that was what they called it.

'Funny old place they have, I hear.'

What had made him say that, she wondered, returning home by taxi. Probably to leave her wondering whether the caravan needed planning permission.

179

*

The switchboard girl reported that Sir Rupert wasn't available. He'd been away all day. Lady Brandish, answering her home phone, told Lorna she had no idea when he'd be back. Now Lorna did need a brandy. She was surprised when at six o'clock he returned her call.

'Mrs Furnival? What can I do for you?'

'You can explain what's going on.'

He gave a sharp laugh. 'Shouldn't I be asking you that?' Today he wasn't bothering with charm. Perhaps when toppled from the platform he'd broken a bone. Was it not a coincidence, she asked him, that these girls had been arrested today?

'Mrs Furnival, I don't know what you're talking about, but for your information the police have, fortunately, apprehended the other two young men involved in my son's death.'

'Fortunately for whom? What young men?'

'I'm told they answer to Mick and Perce,' he said, less with distaste than with amused mockery.

'I don't understand.'

'I can only tell you that they and my son are said to have fallen out that night. Not to mention the girl.'

'First I've heard of it. How do you know? I live closest and I heard nothing.'

'Do you read the local paper?'

'I try not to.'

'It seems that others heard it.'

'What others?'

Silence, intended to reprove her for an improper question?

'They deny it, of course,' he said.

'Why don't you believe them? How do you know all this?'

'I happen to be on the bench.'

'All the more reason—'

'Mrs Furnival,' he interrupted her, 'do I need to remind you that my wife and I are personally involved in this matter? I understand your concern for these young people, but I do ask you to do your best to respect our feelings.'

'Oh not that please,' she wanted to say, but stopped herself and put down the phone.

In the late twilight she stood on her lawn. Close above her head, bats flitted and disappeared. She hadn't seen those for a year or two. Ahead were her trees. Had that empty envelope been some kind of a cry for help? Down through them she went, slithering and swearing. She was close to the caravan before she saw it ahead of her. At first she thought it was empty, then saw a faint yellow line of light. Inside there they were probably using a candle. She approached to knock, but changed her mind and began to struggle up the hill again.

Some hours earlier, at his desk in the *Gazette*'s offices, Keith Haresnip typed fast. Here was real news and *he* had been there.

MINISTER'S CAR SAVAGED. DOOMED VILLAGERS RIOT.

He must hurry. Instead of returning at once to the office he'd made a detour. No one to be seen in the garden of that ridiculous turreted mansion where she lived. He'd stood at the gate, staring up at its drawn curtains. Suddenly one pair had parted and there she'd stood. She'd put out her tongue at him. A couple of seconds later she'd parted them again, grinned and waved. What did she mean, oh what did she mean?

181

Presently he stood in front of the editor's desk.

'What is the day of the week?' the editor enquired.

'Well, Tuesday I think.'

'And if I were to publish this stuff, when would it appear?'

'Friday.'

'So by then it would have been all over the nationals for two whole days.'

'I guess so.'

'That's the sort of thing you must know, not guess, young man.'

The editor read on. ' "Serious injury of an intimate nature." What does that mean?'

'I'm told he was kicked.'

'Where?'

Haresnip sniggered.

'That could be libellous. Did it happen today?'

'I found out today,' Haresnip lied.

'Who is he anyway?'

'He's called Mr Gamble. He owns most of the village.'

'Ah yes, Mr Gamble,' the editor said, and sat back to stare at Haresnip. 'Don't I remember a dog?'

'There isn't anything new about that.'

The editor drew a pad towards him and wrote, then read out, POLICE PLAN RE-ENACTMENT OF MUCH-LOVED REX'S DEATH.'

'Actually its name was Gideon.'

The editor ignored this triviality.

'But how can they do that? Wouldn't they need a look-alike dog? And a look-alike assassin?'

'Exactly,' the editor said. 'You're intrigued, aren't you?'

'But *are* they planning it?'

'I shouldn't think so.'

'Then won't we have to retract?'

'Exactly. That's for the following week. POLICE DENY REX RE-ENACTMENT PLAN. We might even arrange a page of letters from dog lovers.'

'I see.'

'You must try harder, young man.'

'Wanker,' Haresnip murmured, back at his desk.

'Behind closed curtains,' he typed, 'Mr Joseph Cuff, well-known local entrepreneur . . .' then, astonishingly, found himself on the edge of tears.

The following day, a Sunday, when even editors some-times rested and reporters could occasionally please them-selves, Haresnip went again by hired cab to the village. The editor's more threatening words circled in his mind. 'We're not obliged to reveal our sources but I would like to be told. Why? Because I'm being asked.' Succumbing, nevertheless, to temptation, he asked to be dropped at the village's phone box.

She answered. His heart thumped. 'Is that Irma?'

'It is I.'

'This is Keith. You remember? From the *Gazette*. Are you alone? Can you talk?'

'I am thinking so.'

'May I come and interview you?'

'Ha ha. You English call things such funny names.'

He found her on the back lawn, surely even more darkly tanned, wearing only a white tank top vest and white shorts, sitting in an enormous leather armchair.

'Is he away?' Haresnip's knees shook with excitement and to avoid an embarrassing stagger he sat on the edge of another large armchair. 'Your father?'

'Ha ha ha.' She seemed to find that particularly funny. They were getting along famously, Haresnip dared to think. They shared a sense of humour.

183

'He is not well again.'

'In hospital? The same trouble?'

'More bad.' she said, surely with ironic regret.

'Oh dear.'

'They are every day bigger and bigger.'

'Well from one point of view . . .'

'But no more good for using. It is perhaps, how do you say, elephant disease.'

'Oh surely . . .'

'You know what? He thinks not at all of *me* but only – will he be well so he can kill his pheasant birds. Boom boom.' She raised her slim brown arms to sweep the sky with an imaginary gun.

'You think he shot that dog?'

'What dog?'

'Down the road. Your neighbour's.'

'I do not know.'

It was the wrong question. Irma was preoccupied with her own problem.

'You are funny boy,' she said. 'One day I think I shall love you.'

'Oh good.'

'First time you jump on me.'

Haresnip quickly revised his memory of that occasion.

'Now you shake like little baby.'

But Haresnip knew an invitation when he heard one and soon they were naked together in Ralph Gamble's grandfather's four-poster.

Two hours later, fifty yards down the road, Haresnip found those six-foot iron railings chained and padlocked, but, bold with his recent successes, managed to scale them and knock at Mr Joseph Cuff's door. Silence at first, followed by mouse-like scraping noises, then, shockingly close inside, a female voice.

'What do you want?'

'Is Mr Cuff at home?'

'You want my son?'

'I'm from the *Gazette*. I spoke to him before.'

'He is not at home.'

'Perhaps *you* can help me.'

'Who are you? How did you get here?' Rattling sounds of a chain, the door opened two inches and a section of grey face appeared, with a bundle of white hair on top.

'It's quite important. You remember the lad who was drowned?'

'I remember nothing.'

'Mr Cuff heard shouts like a quarrel that evening. Did you hear anything?'

'He tells me nothing.'

'But you might have heard them yourself.'

'If he says there were shouts, of course there were shouts.'

'Yes, yes,' Haresnip said hurriedly, but he was far from satisfied. Interviewing a section of a grey face above a door chain had not been what he'd been trained for. He was more dismayed when, looking down to the bottom of the gap he saw a single sheepskin-lined bedroom slipper and above it the most enormous pink and black ankle he'd ever seen. 'Take a sympathetic interest in their problems,' he remembered one lecturer saying, but to be sympathetically interested in this grotesque limb was more than Haresnip could manage.

'I warn you, boy, if my son finds you here . . .'

The same idea had occurred to Haresnip. His recent confidence was slipping away and the idea of climbing back over those spiked railings while she watched him made him shudder.

'Thank you very much.'

She didn't move.

'I'll say goodbye then.'

No alternative, he returned the way he'd come and managed the climb with only a small tear in his jacket.

Hurrying through the village to phone for a cab, Haresnip passed a succession of printed notices pinned to trees and telegraph poles, but took them for an announcement of some bucolic fiesta. He already had quite enough material on which to base – or invent – a story.

Back at the office, there was an editorial slip of yellow paper stuck to his desk. PLEASE SPEAK. No day of rest for this editor.

'Our discussion yesterday,' he began. 'As a precaution, I'd be grateful if you would confide to me the name of your informant.'

'Of course. A Mr Cuff. Supported by his mother.'

'Owner of the deceased dog.'

'One of them.'

'So there are two now.'

'So I'm told.'

The editor thought about it. Presently, looking down from the ceiling, he said, 'Many thanks, Keith,' causing Haresnip another fright. Never had he realized that the editor might know he had a first name.

'Thank you, sir,' Haresnip said, took a steadying breath of the editor's tobacco fumes and hurried back to his desk.

CHAPTER TWELVE

NOTICES

IN the village, others were more excited by those notices.

'You can take that thing off my fence,' Lorna Furnival told a balding man, the sleeves of his striped shirt held up above the elbows with metal garters.

'That is not among my instructions.'

'You don't say!' Lorna said, making a gash in it with her stick.

'You could be breaking the law.'

Lorna laughed and returned indoors to stand at her window and watch for when he'd finished posting a replacement to strike again.

Elsewhere small groups gathered and peered at the black print.

'They gotta learn to say what they means,' Polly Langridge told one group.

'I'll tell you what the fuckers mean,' Billy Snipe, possible father of three of Shirley Prone's children, explained. 'They means this fuckin' village is done for.'

The sun now high above the trees, some who were late to

hear of the notices were more mystified since, by the time they came to look for them, most lay scattered about in fragments. Fred Fisher, still reflecting on the unfortunate events of the minister's visit, emerged late and missed them entirely as he made for the Red Lion.

One o'clock and the door still locked, he gave it a kick. During his short walk he'd taken an important decision. No longer would he be urbane, reasonable, amiable – though secretly a merry dog. Some might see the minister's visit as a disaster, but surely in fact it had been a last gallant act of defiance in support of a doomed cause, and he had led it. At once he'd walked with shoulders squared, neat black beard thrust forward. He thumped the pub door with his fist and gave it a more violent kick.

The door opened and Wilf Wodge appeared in grubby once-white shirt. 'There's a charge for that,' he said, bending to examine damage to his door before giving Fred a look which said that he resented being woken mid-morning and having his lack of customers exposed.

'Lovely day,' Fred said.

Wilf Wodge stared in bewilderment. Was it possible that someone could be so deluded.

Fred Fisher had still not ordered when the door behind him opened again and Michael Ranch entered.

'Come in there,' Wilf Wodge called, his voice rising in mock astonishment. Two customers within five minutes!

'Have one on me,' Fred Fisher called, and ordered each of them a double whisky with half a pint. 'I owe you an apology,' he said, perching on a stool near the fireplace which he couldn't remember ever seeing alight and tossing down most of his whisky.

'I suppose you do,' Michael Ranch said.

'I *do.*'

'These things happen.'

'No they don't. People make them happen.'

'If you say so.'

'I *do* say so.'

'You mean I should be angry with you.'

'That's right. Why aren't you?'

Michael Ranch sipped his whisky. 'Because we're both in the same boat.'

This was news to Fred. Surely not his wife, Wendy, having it off with poor, cuckolded Michael Ranch.

'In what sense?'

'Both of us deserted.'

Michael Ranch described his wife's flight which, although quickly abandoned, seemed to represent something final.

'Well I'm damned,' Fred Fisher said. 'Will she come back?'

'Who knows.' What Michael was not going to reveal was that he, unlike poor Fred, was consoling himself at 2 Keats Villas.

'Have this one on me,' he said, assembling the glasses with his long pale fingers and carrying them to the bar.

For some while they sat in silence in front of the fireplace, both absorbing what they had learned, both alternately sipping whisky and beer.

'Where do we go from here?' Fred Fisher said.

'Ask me another.'

'You could call it a proper fuck up,' Fred said.

They both found this rather funny.

'You seen these notices?' Michael Ranch asked.

'What notices?'

'Nor have I,' he said. This, too, seemed so witty that Fred glanced respectfully at Michael Ranch.

189

'You know, I like you,' Fred Fisher said. They were standing side by side in the Red Lion's urinals, and Fred gave Michael's shoulder a playful shove, making him spray his shoes.

'I like you,' Michael Ranch said, and might have done the same if Fred had not dodged one urinal along.

'Me too.'

'Never expected to,' Fred said.

'Nor did I.'

They returned to the bar and sat looking at their empty glasses.

'One for the road?' Michael suggested, and at the same moment saw an apparently unsupported head above the bar, grinning at him between two beer mugs. Not usually a pub-goer, he had heard of Joan Wodge but never actually seen her and, for a second, thought such an unusual amount of whisky might be responsible.

'Two for the road,' Fred Fisher corrected him.

'I hadn't meant to tell you,' Michael Ranch said, and revealed his love for Mrs Prone.

'Glory be!' Fred Fisher said, staring at Michael with new respect, and bought them both a round of drinks.

'Funny thing,' Fred said. 'It's a sort of relief.' Relief, he had meant, from his guilt about Virginia, which much whisky before lunch had suddenly made so real.

'Know what you mean,' Michael said, referring to the convenient freedom his wife's illness had been allowing him.

'Speaking of those notices,' Fred said.

'The ones you *haven't* seen.'

'The point is,' Fred began. He knew he had one, but it had suddenly slipped away. 'Ah yes, the point is, we can't speak sensibly about them unless we find them.'

'Indeed.'

'And read them.'

They rose, both a little unsteadily.

'Nice to have met you,' Wilf Wodge said.

'Sarcastic bugger,' Fred Fisher said.

Together they helped each other out into the dazzling sunlight, and began to lurch down Red Lion Lane towards the village street.

'Watch your step.'

'Watch yours.'

Presently they began to see them, mostly by now blown into ditches. At the same moment both saw a yellow one which they both liked the look of.

'I saw it.'

'No you didn't.'

In the ensuing struggle they each secured about half the A4 sheet.

'Too dark,' Fred said, holding it out to the brilliant sunlight.' I shall take it home and study it at my leisure. Legal training always comes in useful.' Fred had once started an evening class in company law.

'Toss you for the balance,' Michael Ranch said, but the coin landed in long grass and they couldn't find it.

'Double or quits,' Fred Fisher said, but neither of them understood what was at stake and both began to giggle.

'You're a good bloke,' Fred Fisher said.

They shook hands. Michael Ranch would have liked to say the same, but needed to lean against a nearby garden fence to help him control a shameful need to vomit.

'What's that?' Wendy Fisher asked Fred, as she encouraged her fourth child upstairs with a whack on its plastic nappy.

'Just something I picked up,' Fred told her, hiding the

191

yellow fragment and retiring to his desk. Here he read:

GIRLS FRIENDLY . . .
Final meeting will be . . .
due to circumstances beyond . . .
Warmest thanks to all concerned . . .
Signed
Revd. Charles . . .

A moment later Wendy arrived to set a fragment of a white notice on his desk. 'Something which might interest you . . .'

Later that night Fred Fisher improved, signed, sealed and stamped letters which till now he'd prevented himself sending.

Dear Sir Rupert

We are all saddened to hear of the injury you suffered during the recent visit of the Minister for the Environment. If our feelings about the proposed Road Plan and future development of our village were so strong that they got out of hand I must ask your pardon. None of us doubt that you have worked hard to bring this disastrous project to a successful conclusion, so destroying our picturesque, indeed historic . . .

Watch it, Fred cautioned himself, but tonight he was beyond caution.

Dear Minister

We are all deeply grateful to you for the way you recently spared us a few minutes of your valuable time to explain so enticingly the prospect which lies ahead for this village. How well your government is keeping its promise to protect the countryside. I do not have to tell you how keenly we, as a small and backward community, look forward to our obliteration. . . .'

Later he composed and duplicated a notice of his own

NO SURRENDER TO BUREAUCRATIC VANDALS
Today we have learned . . .
Now is the time . . .

At around midnight, letters, notices and drawing pins in a bag, he returned to the village street and, under a brilliant moon, managed to post the letters and pin up half-a-dozen notices – rather crookedly – before a headache drove him home.

Elsewhere many in the village had found other ways to face the future. Back at the Red Lion, Wilf Wodge was sharing a nightcap with Evan Mullins.

'Pissed as bleeding arseholes,' Wilf Wodge said, referring to his two lunchtime customers.

'Doesn't surprise me,' Evan Mullins said, though whether about the dissipated lives of those in authority or the fragment of white A4 he held in one hand seemed uncertain.

COUNTY ROAD PLAN PROJECT
WARNING OF TREE FELLING AND SITE CLEARANCE

'So it's all stitched up,' Wilf Wodge said.
'That's what it looks like.'
'Well well,' Evan Mullins said. So set in pessimism were they both that they seemed to have no words for such a satisfactory development.

A hundred yards away Lorna Furnival watched the high-lights of Newcastle's latest defeat, jabbing the floor with her stick at the manager's incompetence.

At the other end of the village Ernest Boon set an illegal snare, hoarded for years in his shed, on the main cat track across his garden. Using a wooden mallet wrapped in a tea towel he thumped the anchor peg into the ground. Long before dawn he would be out with a spade to bury any success. Perhaps he should bring the mallet too, in case last rites were required. Indoors, he checked the downstairs rooms to be sure he hadn't been observed. Tiffany must be upstairs, though there was silence up there. Suppose she was again on her way to Auckland. That afternoon he'd ventured down Chestnut Lane then across fields to the edge of Lorna's wood, hoping for at least a glimpse of Briony. Through trees he'd seen that caravan, but no sign of its occupants. Once it had seemed to rock – hardly likely since it was without wheels and firmly bedded into the ground, though possible, given Briony's weight. He'd returned the same way, disappointed but also relieved. If she'd emerged, how would he have explained himself? Bird spotting? He doubted if she would have believed him. Just a pathetic peeping Tom, she would have thought. His cowardice saddened him. There might not be many more opportuni-ties.

Two hundred yards further into the country, Irma Svenson stood naked in front of a long mirror admiring herself as she experimented with different angles for her arms and hips, occasionally pausing to anoint the injuries which Haresnip in his boyish enthusiasm had inflicted on her. Seven miles away, Ralph Gamble groaned in his hospi-tal bed, partly with pain, partly at the Road Plan, partly at the thought that his injury might hasten the day when Irma would leave him.

As dusk came, Admiral Jack Hawker and Anne Hawker played racing demon. It was many years since they'd done this, but they were pleased to find that they had retained some of their youthful skills. Their old hands flew here and there across the table and occasional cards flew down on to the carpet. Soon they were quite breathless.

'You think we should up anchor and away?' the admiral said.

'I know whose neck I'd wring first, the snivelling little hypocrite,' Anne Hawker said.

She was thinking of Mr Fisher, the admiral knew, and noticed that her hands were clenching and unclenching as if practising this execution.

In their woodland caravan, Foxglove tucked up, Briony Hawker and Sandra played other games. From hugging they had long ago moved to kissing, then more intimate fumbling. It was their troubles, they half realized, which had led them to invent more daring diversions. They'd also settled their diet differences, Sandra occasionally managing a tinned sardine without thinking of the poor little creature trapped by the gills and wriggling in a fisherman's net, while Briony had come to quite enjoy the tingling in the stomach which nettle soup gave her. Sandra had gained ten pounds in weight and Briony had lost two. Tonight, temporarily exhausted by their play, they sat partially wrapped in blankets, staring at what they could see of each other's lovely nakedness, bright eyed with astonishment at their own naughtiness.

'Will they take the caravan away?' Sandra asked.

'They'll have to take us too,' Briony said.

Mrs Volga was making soup of another kind, using her own time-saving method. You simply put all the vegetables

THOMAS HINDE

into the pot unwashed and, as they cooked, the earth and stones sank to the bottom. Tomorrow she would take some of this brew to Mr Taylor in a thermos. He needed comforting. She hardly dared tell him that the motorway down the valley was now planned to have a slip road just beyond the ridge, easily within sound and smell if not actual sight of his garden. Fumes, vibration, noise all night.

'Plants need sleep as much as humans,' he'd explained to her.

At 2 Keats Villas Michael Ranch was in disgrace.

'You drunken sod,' Shirley Prone had greeted him, experienced at noticing unsteady walks.

Michael Ranch had retired to the toilet where he'd made horrible noises now trying but failing to be sick.

'Feeling better?' Shirley Prone asked.

'Bit.'

'Well you'll just have to wait till I get this lot out of the way.' She jerked her head towards her children and was annoyed to be able to count only five.

So Michael Ranch watched the television, listened to the yells and crashes of those who had been dragged away from it, and waited hopefully. Was it the news of the final destruction of the village that made him both desperate and more than usually randy? he wondered.

Down Chestnut Lane his own home was dark and silent.

At about the same time Polly Langridge was looking at her book of village photos. 'I'll be blowed if that's not old Mr Gamble,' she said, holding it up to the light. Sam Langridge sat on the settee, wriggling his released and sockless toes. 'Nonsense,' he said, without looking.

'I'd know his hat anywhere. Remember the bees he kept? Remember how he got half-a-dozen of 'em in that net thing he put round his head and went running one end of the village to the other?'

Sam exercised his bulbous toes.

'One end to the other he run, 'ollerin fit to bust.' Her eyes grew misty. 'That's one thing they can't take away from us: our memories.'

'Nonsense,' Sam said.

Down Farm Lane, Gertie Jones and Geoff Riddle stood together in Geoff's barn, using Geoff's paraffin lamp to see Geoff's donkey. Moses lay on his side. Every half minute its rib cage gave a convulsive heave.

'Reckon he's on his way out,' Geoff said.

'Could be right.'

'Been a friend for fifteen years.'

To her amazement Gertie realized that tears were running down Geoff's face. Vertically, just like anyone else's. Somehow his squint would have made her expect one lot to take a different course.

'You soppy old thing.'

Presently they were sitting side by side on the floor, their backs against a hay bale. Cautiously Gertie reached out a hand to take Geoff's. To hide the embarrassment this caused her she gave a simultaneous yell, 'You be quiet in there', pretending she'd heard Tobias kicking his bucket around.

Geoff wiped his eyes on his coat sleeve.

'We could send for the vet, give him a drench,' Gertie said, referring to the donkey.

'And what would that cost?'

'I wouldn't bother.'

She squeezed his hand. For the first time in her life she found herself fancying a biped – well, not quite the first, there had been poor Bob Brandish, but that had had more to do with the ring in his nose.

'He's lucky in a way,' Geoff said, about the donkey again.

197

'How's that?'

'He won't see what we'll see. No trees to rub against.'

'Come off it, Geoff, you don't go rubbing yourself against them,' she said, pretending to misunderstand.

'You don't know what I do.'

They laughed a lot.

After a while they began to biff each other in a friendly but increasingly exciting way.

'Oo!'

'Ouch!'

'Shall we?'

'Well, don't matter what we do now, does it?'

'What about him?' – Moses.

'He wouldn't object, poor old thing.'

The hay was prickly but Gertie rather liked that and at the climax gave such a squeal that Tobias stopped kicking his stable wall to listen.

Some hours earlier Joseph Cuff had driven back through the village at defiant speed. During the day he'd shouted at his business partner and dismissed his secretary. That would teach them. All the way home he remembered it with satisfaction.

Slithering to a halt outside his chained gates he realized once again that there would be no Gideon to leap as high as his head and try to bite his ears.

'Home, Mumsie.'

No answer. One day there would never again be an answer. Not today because there she was, standing quite still at the top of the stairs, staring down at him.

'About time too, Joseph,' she said.

Jo Cuff retired to the kitchen. No need to check his study desk. The letter informing him that he was to be charged with dangerous driving would still be there.

In the upstairs room of her cottage, Miss Wiggum slept restlessly despite the help of Temazepan. She had also received a letter. Her job no longer existed. The school would not reopen in September. An additional daily bus would collect and remove the village's primary school-children. The arrangement was probably only temporary, the letter pretended to comforted her. In due course a modern and more appropriate primary school, able to accommodate up to a dozen times as many children, would be built to provide for the children of a number of villages and lead to substantial economies, a development which would be made possible by the County Road Plan.

199

CHAPTER THIRTEEN

YELLOW MEN

THE weather broke. Rain swept up the valley, carried on a wind which set the trees swaying and tossing. Later they stood still and dripped. It was Lorna Furnival's weather, had been since she was a child.

With the rain came men in yellow jackets. They were to be seen everywhere about the village, examining plans held at arm's length, knocking red-topped marker posts into the ground. One line ran beyond the ridge above the village where four months ago that first yellow machine had been seen by many in the village, and damaged by the Prone children. Now several vast machines were parked there with a dog in the cab of one.

The young Prones did not repeat their investigations, as if they sensed that the whole village was losing hope and the time for cheeky vandalism had passed, though more probably because Justin was told by his mother that if he started another stomach epidemic she'd knock him senseless. Nor did Gertie Jones take Tobias up there to see what was happening, remembering what a single yellow machine had done to his nerves. Bad enough that the day after her night in the hay with Geoff Riddle the animal had tossed her off.

'Don't you tell me he didn't know,' she told Geoff.

'Could be coincidence,' Geoff told her.

'I've heard it called some funny things.'

'You're saying he knew what we was up to.'

'Of course he knew.'

A simpler explanation was that Gertie, in celebration, had put Tobias at a five-foot thorn hedge and he'd come to an abrupt halt, sending her flying to its far side.

More mysterious was the disappearance of Moses. He'd simply gone from the place in the barn where he'd been lying. For several days Geoff hunted.

'You seen a stray donkey?' he asked a man in a yellow jacket.

'What's that?'

'D-O-N-K-E-Y.'

'I seen plenty of them these last few days.'

Eventually Geoff found him lying on his side at the bottom of the twenty acre – a huge sodden balloon, his hair no longer properly covering his belly so that streaks of grey skin showed.

'Wanted to die by himself,' Geoff told Gertie.

'You don't think someone did it?'

Geoff shrugged. 'You saying someone led him there? He wouldn't have gone, not with a stranger.'

That morning Geoff had set about unburying his gun – but the rain had so spread the miden that he'd little idea where to dig and after an hour, smelly and frustrated, had given up.

The main line of red-topped stakes now defined the road's southern route along the valley below Lorna's wood, then across Joseph Cuff's meadow and close by Ralph

Gamble's pheasant-raising cages.

'Waiting for the word "Go",' one of the few men prepared to talk told Lorna, who had struggled down her wooded hillside in a mackintosh under an umbrella to see what was happening. He was a jovial fellow, with large beer belly which, together with his round white helmet, made him suggest Humpty Dumpty.

'I'll tell you where to go,' Lorna said. Her large pointed nose dripped.

The man laughed.

'You've chosen some nice solid ground,' she suggested. The lines of posts ran between the two deepest of her black ponds.

'We'll soon fill those.'

'Some of you could end up filling them yourselves.' It was an empty threat and they both knew it.

'Thanks for the warning, Mrs Furnival.'

However did he know her name?

One drenching morning Sir Rupert Brandish phoned Fred Fisher. 'I shall not be taking any action with respect to your recent letter.'

'That's kind of you, Sir Rupert.'

'On the other hand you'd be well advised to remember that libel is not confined to publicly printed matter.'

'I appreciate your advice, Sir Rupert.'

Wasted sarcasm, Fred reflected, and continued to strut about the village, often below an umbrella, sure that he was a changed man. He wasn't even dismayed when his wife reported that she was pregnant for the sixth time.

'You always were a joker,' he told her.

But within seconds he'd been visited by a comforting family group of the future: Frederick Fisher surrounded by not less than half-a-dozen offspring, impoverished but defiant to the last.

In these days – it was early August – Sam Langridge not only continued to swab out the village's public toilet but began to bring to the job his six-foot mop. Jabbing fiercely with this weapon, he broke the cement which fixed the porcelain bowl to the tiles, so rupturing the seal between the S-bend and the sewage pipe – an accident which, after a moment's worry, made him laugh loudly. Now, when the chain was pulled a trickle of filthy water ran out under the toilet's door and down one side of the village street, so discouraging the contractor's workmen.

'They can fucking use the bushes,' Sam told Polly. 'It weren't built for them. That were done by public subscription, for us to relieve ourselves when we fancy.'

'You can say that again.'

'Not day after day, not one after another. Reckon it was all that extra weight what broke it.'

Polly nodded. She was emptying her flour bin, concealing from Sam a colony of weevils she'd discovered at its bottom.

'Fact you could say it's them not me should mend it,' Sam concluded.

'Pancakes,' Polly said. 'That's what we be having. Same as Lent. Using up the left overs such as would rot. Well, wouldn't you?'

Sam was thinking of sewage gas.

'Those Israelis is too clever for their own good. I don't blame them Arabs having it in for them. What *we* need is a bomb or two, not to mention some of them suicide chappies.'

Not now fancying the village's public lavatories, the workmen used the Gents at the Red Lion, filling Wilfred Wodge with fury since some of them didn't even buy his sandwiches. To the contents of these he cautiously added local products, for example crushed slugs caught on the kitchen tiles, and dandelion leaves, knowing the effect these last were supposed to have. And they did, judging by the way more and more came to use the Red Lion's facilities. To keep them guessing he still filled other sandwiches with cooking margarine, very thin sliced ham and unusually hot mustard.

'Now they're asking for pickle,' he told Evan Mullins one grey evening. 'Who do they think they are?'

He'd called on Evan, leaving Joan behind the bar, so that he could complain about the ridiculously small profit he was making on this enterprise and at the same time allow Evan to guess that these well-paid workmen were paying through the nose, so making a nice contribution to his takings. Evan Mullins could tell from the way his friend went on and on about his miserable sandwiches, and was furious. Now Evan not only hated all those mean sods who'd ruined his own business, but even more viciously all those bastards who were supporting his supposed friend. If only he'd kept his shop open.

Mrs Volga, meanwhile, had made a discovery which vindicated her opinion of the unfeeling people among whom she was compelled to live. Arriving one morning at Mr Taylor's with a summer cake – blackcurrants, radishes and potatoes baked in birch bark – she'd found his door locked and been unable to rouse him. First she'd circled his house, peering through windows and seen one or two chairs lying on their sides. That was strange. Then she'd stumbled about the ruined garden and discovered several empty cartons labelled Weed Killer and a red watering-can with a chemical smell.

In this emergency she hurried to Admiral Hawker, who

she couldn't help respecting as a gallant seaman.

'I think he is doing something stupid.'

'Tulips? Wrong time of year.'

'I think first he kills his garden then he kills himself.'

'You do? Damned shame. Anne, listen to this.'

Together the three of them returned to Mr Taylor's garden, sniffed the watering can and peered through the house windows.

'We must break him down,' Mrs Volga said. 'His big door.'

But Admiral Hawker retained a dislike of doing anything without orders from above, instilled sixty years ago at Dartmouth Naval College where any tendency towards Nelsonian behaviour had been crushed, and asked his wife to call the police.

An hour later they came, along with a locksmith and went from room to room of the small house. Apart from those two overturned kitchen chairs, all was tidy. Mr Taylor was nowhere to be found.

They returned to the station and filed a report. In the following days this went from desk to desk, eventually reaching the officer who had prepared the reckless-driving submission to the CPS, who presently realized that he'd lost a key witness.

The news that he was not to be prosecuted soon reached Mr Joseph Cuff who started to tell his mother before remembering he'd never mentioned the matter to her. So what? He'd create a scene about her failing memory.

'Aren't you pleased, Mumsie?'

For several minutes they shouted at each other with growing enjoyment, he from the front hall below the portrait of his grandmother, she from the top of the stairs. There was a bad moment when she seemed about to attempt to come down to his level, still making him expect a blow, as he'd often done for forty years.

'Be careful,' he yelled.

That stopped her. 'Joseph, you are a silly boy and you tell big lies,' she said, and retired to her bedroom.

It was a few days later, but apparently unconnected, that other policemen and a policewoman came to Lorna's caravan but failed to find Sandra Moss, as Briony had decided she should be called.

'Get off your backside,' Lorna wanted to tell him, 'if you can.' She was phoning her solicitor, Mr Vivian Mountjoy, pictured him struggling to rise, but unable to detach his jacket from his swivel chair.

'They may not find her, but if they do I'd like you to be there.' 'This time,' she avoided adding. 'Tell her to say *nothing*. Make sure she understands. Frighten her more than the police. Frighten them too if you can. Tell her on no account ever to sign anything. And incidentally find out what it's all about.'

She could hear his disapproving silence, picture his shiny silver hair and switch-on, switch-off smile.

In fact, she was fairly sure the police wouldn't find her because she'd been ahead of them, Sandra and her child, along with Briony Hawker, now living in her garden room, the duck in her tool shed. Sooner or later they'd anyway have had to leave the caravan. The new road would run only ten yards below.

Now there was something more difficult, which she was less sure she could manage. Among old newspapers she found a copy of *Town Ad*. Nothing under 'P', she tried the Yellow Pages: YOUR FRIENDLY PLUMBER.

She phoned. 'Is that my friendly plumber?'

'You don't want to believe all you read.'

'I need your help. It's urgent.'

'It always is, specially on Sundays.'

'Could I come and see you? To explain.'

The suggestion seemed to confuse him.

'All right, you come here,' she said.

'I reckon that might be better like. Let's see, not next week, not the week after . . .'

'No no . . .' Or was he joking? What could she say to persuade him? 'Tonight,' she said, but without much hope.

Several seconds passed. 'OK,' he said.

He was a dark, unshaven young man in a black baseball cap, with broken front teeth.

'Nice little pad you got,' he said, helping himself to a view across her lawn.

'Not for much longer.'

'So I hear.'

She told him her problem. He listened and said nothing, giving her the dismaying sense that it was she who was being judged.

'He drowned, you say.'

'That's right.'

'And these folk had a hose down there for water?'

She nodded.

'And people have been putting two and two together. And where was this hose found?'

'Luckily no one seems to remember.'

'But the hole they were digging was full of water.'

'Full enough.'

'So if this water didn't come from the hose, where did it come from?'

'I've no idea. I only want it to be certain that it didn't come from the hose.'

He said nothing, but gave her a long stare.

'The whole place down there is a bog. It could have seeped in anywhere. He may have diverted an underground stream.'

He went on staring at her. Presently he said, 'I'm not asking why you want this.'

'Good. Could you have been doing some work here that day? Perhaps you'd needed to disconnect it.'

'Oh there's ways,' he said.

So at least that didn't seem to be a problem.

'The police get funny ideas.'

'Ah, them.'

By luck she seemed to have scored. It gave her courage for the most difficult question. 'I'll make it worth your while,' she said, but she was out of her depth, suspected this was slang from some long-ago film thriller.

'Five hundred,' he said. Not a moment's hesitation. Would she have liked him better if he'd asked nothing? No, was the answer. She was close to tears of gratitude.

'What makes you think it wasn't her?'

'I just know. She isn't that sort of person.'

Presently he left. 'Let you know,' he said.

An hour later he phoned. 'You see, there's my books,' he said. 'If I was to fiddle them and it showed, that could finish me.'

'I understand.'

'I got a kid, did I mention?' he said. 'And the wife,' he added, as an afterthought.

'I quite understand.'

It was 10 p.m. when her doorbell rang. 'There's a few things to fix,' he said. 'Needs to be gravity fed. Better not to have to explain shutting off the mains.'

For an hour he worked while she made him tea and drank Horlicks.

'I'll let you have the paperwork in the morning. There'll be an invoice for a new tank. Forget that. It'll say "paid".'

Vivian Mountjoy phoned her the next day to explain the likely charge.

'But that's completely impossible.' She was learning – managed to sound genuinely amazed.

'Not as they see it. They're holding those other two young men, who seem to have said unwise things.'

'I tell you, it's just not possible. That was one of the days there wasn't any water.'

'You mean the mains?'

'I mean the supply from the garden tap to that hose. It was gravity fed.' But she mustn't show unlikely under-standing. 'I was having a new tank and connection. If I look I can probably find the bills and dates.'

'No doubt in court . . .'

'But it mustn't come to court. Surely if they knew there'd be no charge.'

Silence. She suspected he wasn't believing her, but perhaps that didn't matter.

'I think you'd better find those invoices and let me see them.'

Early that afternoon she took them by taxi to his office.

She tried to sleep but couldn't. She was more shaken than she'd expected. I don't believe in punishment, she told herself. Those who punish, punish themselves. Who had said that?

The sun appeared again – tentatively, as if it hadn't quite made up its mind, Lorna thought, but nevertheless ventured on to her wet lawn. And there they were, clearly to be seen through the windows of her garden room, the child propped against a box, Sandra on her knees facing it, probably cooing at it. Children was what they both were.

Lorna waved to them, and at the same moment admitted what she'd been hiding from herself: she had unfinished business.

The girl opened the door, then hurried back to stop the child toppling sideways.

'Did you send me a letter?' Lorna asked.

No answer. She wouldn't even look up, now busy settling the baby on the lower bunk bed.

'I just wondered. I got an empty envelope.'

'It got lost,' the girl said, still speaking towards the child.

'Did you want to tell me something?'

Now there were tears. '. . . tell someone . . .' Lorna thought she heard.

'It's none of my business,' Lorna said – true, though far too late to admit.

'I don't know, oh I don't know.'

Lorna waited till the sobbing stopped.

'Would it help if you told me? You needn't worry. I'd never mention it.'

More sobs.

'Let's start with the hose.'

'It was there already,' she said.

'Already in the hole?'

She nodded.

A lie? Lorna had no idea.

'He'd been so horrid. He wanted to kill her.'

'The duckling?'

She nodded.

'But if you found it there, why didn't you pull it out?'

'I tried. It wouldn't come. I think the tap was jammed on something.'

Certainly it had had a clumsy tap on the end.

'Couldn't you have cut through it?'

Silence. 'I never thought . . .'

That also sounded likely.

'Now listen to me carefully,' Lorna said. 'The hose wasn't working that day. All right? It had been cut off the whole day.'

She didn't answer, just stared with teary eyes.

'You couldn't possibly have forgotten because it was so inconvenient, having no water.' She stared at the girl, wondering if there was any better way to impress her.

'There it is then. I'm just telling you in case you're asked. With luck you won't be. Cheer up. The sun's trying to shine.'

CHAPTER FOURTEEN

END OF THE ROAD

BY the end of August a date had been fixed: 15 September.

DOOMED VILLAGE HEARS ITS FATE Keith Haresnip composed, and was given permission to collect heart-rending stories.

Boldly he stood in Mr Gamble's porch and tugged the iron bell rod. Irma came quickly, wearing a scarlet bath cap on one side of her head like a beret and white cotton shorts like a schoolboy footballer.

'Fuck me, it is you!' She seemed pleased with her growing vocabulary.

'May I come in?'

'Not this day.'

'Oh dear.'

She gestured upwards with a thumb.

'He's come home? Should we be talking like this?'

'Do not worry. He sleeps.'

'At ten in the morning? Is it because of the news? Is he depressed?' *Village senior citizen sinks into melancholia.*

'He is sad. No, that is not why.'

'What is it then?'

'You have English song, yes? About green bottles, yes? Now he has just one.'

'In the song there were ten at first.'

'I do not understand. He never has ten.'

'So they've amputated one and sent him home?'

'I am nursemaid. I give him pills and bandage.'

'So we have a problem.'

'Perhaps.' She turned her head sideways and looked at him out of the corners of her eyes. 'Perhaps one day I give him two, three pills. He sleeps long time.'

Disappointed, Haresnip roamed the village in search of inspiration and was lucky enough to be passed by Fred Fisher. They recognized each other and Fred braked. Peering into his car, Haresnip saw that there was a load of some sort on the back seat, covered by sacking.

'Preparing for a tactical withdrawal?' he suggested provocatively.

'Certainly not,' Fred said.

He had in fact been to the town's agricultural merchant where he'd demanded heavy-duty chain, 'cut into lengths'.

'Of, say, seven foot, eight foot?' the salesman asked.

'No no, shorter.' But how much shorter Fred wasn't sure.

'What would be their purpose, if I may ask, sir?'

'Five foot,' Fred said. It would depend, of course, on the size of each trunk, as well as of the person. 'And the same number of heavy duty padlocks.'

'They don't come cheap.'

'Invoice the parish council,' Fred told him with careless bravado.

'A little surprise for our friends,' he now told Haresnip, and drove on to prevent himself revealing more.

Back at his desk, Haresnip, more observant than Fred had supposed, worked on a suitably emotive piece.

Gathered in little knots, they stood about the village street, planning their last stand. 'We shall go down with our flag flying,' declaimed Mr Frederick Fisher, their self-appointed leader, as he laboured at assembling and chaining together a barrier made from ancient farm wagons not seen for half a century. From his sick bed, Mr Ralph Gamble, owner of extensive village property, announced his intention of going on hunger strike. Next Sunday the much loved Reverend Charles Sage – Charlie to villagers – will conduct a symbolic funeral service among the village's ancient tombstones. At the Red Lion, publican Wilfred Wodge has a number of herbal additives which he is using to flavour the beer he serves to any construction worker rash enough to sample it . . .

His work was not printed.

'What's this out-of-date crap?' the editor asked, and told him to turn his attention to the disappearance of Wong, a prize-winning Burmese cat, latest victim of a gang of cat kidnappers active in the neighbourhood. Anyone who saw men or women marked by unusual scratches should contact the police.

In the village Fred distributed his chains.

'On Battle of Britain day!' he explained. 'Isn't that an omen?'

'You mean. . . ?'

'Further orders will follow.'

'You'll be wanting us to. . . ?'

'Depending on where the first attack materializes.'

'What if it rains?'

'Good question,' Fred said, and drove on.

This was also the first day of the new school term. That morning the younger children had assembled in front of the closed village school to be driven away – though fewer than usual, now some families had accepted compulsory purchase offers for their houses and left the village. Also missing were some who should have been there, including the four Prone children who were of school age: Justin, Karen, Winston and Howard. If Shirley knew where they were she wasn't saying.

'For all new children, their first day at a school is of particular importance,' the new school secretary told Mrs Prone on the phone.

'What do you expect me to do about it?'

The school secretary wasn't sure. 'You could search for them.'

'What do I do with the others I'd like to know?'

'Are there more!' the school secretary accidentally allowed herself to exclaim.

'You're telling me there are.'

It was mid-afternoon when Justin showed himself. Though the sun sometimes shone, a blustery wind blew and heavy clouds raced overhead as he slipped through Miss Wiggum's garden gate and stood knocking at her kitchen door, glancing occasionally over his shoulder.

'Who is it?'

'It's me, miss.'

Justin heard shuffling feet, the turning of a key.

'Justin!'

Still glancing over his shoulder, Justin edged forward and was presently inside.

'Why aren't you at school?'

215

'It's like this, Miss Wiggum, the bus din come to the right place.'

'Didn't it?'

'Not where we was 'specting it.'

'Perhaps *you* were in the wrong place.'

The subject didn't interest Justin, who let it lapse. 'You see, Miss Wiggum, seeing as you was leaving—'

'I've not been well, Justin.'

'—there's somefin we reckons we oughter tell you.'

'There is?'

'You know that dorg what copped it?'

'Justin, I don't think you should go on.'

'Well, me and me bruvvers reckons—'

'Justin, whatever it is you have to say, it could be better I don't hear.'

'You do, miss?'

'I do, Justin.'

She longed to tell him to continue. Tears ran down her cheeks and she ignored them, hoping he wouldn't notice.

'All right, miss, if that's how you wants it.'

For a moment they were both silent.

'There's somefin else, Miss Wiggum. Seen you're retirin' like, we thought we'd bring you somefin. A present like.'

'Justin, you shouldn't.'

'It's from me bruvvers and sister too.'

'Did they also miss the bus?'

'Last I seed 'em they was be'ind the hedge.'

'My hedge?'

Justin nodded and at the same time produced what he had been hiding behind his back: a two-pound jam jar dangling from a loop of string, half full of murky black water in which live things stirred.

'Whatever is it, Justin?' She saw a flash of orange.

216

'It's some of those nooty things what you teached us about.'

' "Taught" Justin. Where did you get them?'

'Ponds and places. There's Mrs Furnival's ponds. She don't mind.'

'Oh, Justin, I don't know what to say.'

'You don't need to say nuffin, Miss Wiggum. The thing is, you don't need to keep 'em if you don't want. Just put 'em in the sink and when you've had enough you scoops 'em up wiv a tea cup like and lets 'em go. Me sister said you'd like 'em 'cos they was pretty things,' Justin said, and ran away, down the garden path, out through the garden gate. Here his two brothers and sister were already running away and he followed them, punching them if he ever got close enough.

It was an hour later that Fred Fisher stopped in front of Miss Wiggum's cottage, sorted a length of chain and a padlock from the heap on his back seat and carried them up her garden path. Miss Wiggum was unwell, he knew, and he hardly expected her to join in what he thought of as the village's final act of defiance. On the other hand, her life had been more completely wrecked by the Plan than anyone else's and she might have been hurt if he'd forgotten to offer her the chance.

'Come in,' she called, with a robustness he hadn't expected. What he discovered was also unexpected. She gave him only a glance before, standing at her kitchen table, she continued to peer through a magnifying glass into a white plastic washing-up bowl. She was wearing a plastic apron over a man's woollen dressing-gown.

Fred laid his heavy chain by the door and came closer to peer with her. In the bowl, flipping about in some muddy water, he saw half a dozen newts – but like no newts he'd

217

seen before, almost twice the size, with dragon-like spines and vivid orange and yellow bellies.

'Look at *them*!' Fred said. 'Never met that sort.'

Miss Wiggum, he now saw, had open beside the bowl what looked like a children's natural history encyclopaedia. In turn she peered at this then back at the bowl.

'Where did *they* come from?'

'A present.'

'Funny kind of present.'

'Retirement.' But she wasn't properly listening. 'That's them,' she said, putting a thick finger on an illustration in the book, looking up at him as if noticing him for the first time. 'Rare, arguably unknown in the South-East,' she quoted.

She rose from the table, fetched a china jug from her sink and went into the garden where she could be glimpsed sploshing about in a rainwater butt. Fred took the opportunity to recover his chain and padlock from the doormat and hide them inside the flaps of his raincoat. He'd been right to be worried about this call. Miss Wiggum was apparently suffering regression to childhood. To ask her to padlock herself to a tree would not be right.

'Bye then.'

But the story was too good for Fred to keep to himself. Besides, it demonstrated the way in which the Plan would not only destroy a unique landscape and a living community, but was already causing personal tragedies. Ten minutes later, making his next call, he was explaining this to Ernest Boon, among the incidental tables of his front room.

'Poor old girl's quite a sight. So excited her grey curls dangling into a bowl of filthy water.' Fred was no longer particular about improving a tale.

'What species did you say?' Ernest asked.

Fred named it.

Ernest Boon became absent-minded, accepting his chain and padlock – and one of each for Tiffany – without apparent reluctance. It was only gradually as Fred continued to improve his tale that he realized Ernest was staring at him in an odd way, tufts of hair rising almost vertically above his ears.

'*Protected species.*'

'Is that so?'

'*Protected habitat.*'

Together they hurried across the road, past the church to Lorna Furnival's, where they knocked with excited impatience on her door. Inside she heard them dimly. She was exhausted and depressed.

'I'm a member of the RSPB,' Ernest said. 'Have been for thirty-three years.'

'Whatever they are, it doesn't sound as if they're birds,' Lorna said.

'I've met the president,' Ernest said, forgetting to add "eleven years ago". 'He'd know who could advise us.'

It was still only four o'clock. 'We should at least take soundings,' Fred said.

With increasing excitement which she found hard to control, Lorna made phone calls, was provoked by protective secretaries with lies about meetings, shouted at them, demanding home numbers.

Next day the calls multiplied, grew longer and became of still greater interest, until, slowly, to the amazement of all, they became positively encouraging. Faxes went here and there, letters were carried by motor-cycle messengers, ecological societies were consulted, lawyers briefed, learned judges required to give opinions, until, within ten days, the magic words were whispered: ON HOLD.

At first tentatively, then with increasing confidence, the villagers, each in his or her own way celebrated.

Geoff Riddle bought a new donkey, which he named Mr Prick. Since he and Gertie Jones continued what they had surprised themselves by starting, Fred Fisher began to describe goings on at the Riddle farm as Animal Crackers.

Polly and Sam Langridge composed a complaint to the council about damage done to the village public toilets by visiting workmen, to which the council spitefully replied that closure and demolition would be cheaper than repairing them, usefully reducing the council's wage bill.

Ernest Boon, who, even before the reprieve, had been taking ancient tins of condensed milk, stolen from Tiffany's atomic-war reserve, to Sandra and Briony, now asked them whether Foxglove would like a godfather. Relaxing in deck chairs of ancient, finger-crushing design, not erected since Harry Furnival's death, they seemed not to know what to say. The moment he'd spoken Ernest realized that his proposal was an admission that he would never come any closer to the girl he was in love with, but at the same time that it might be a nostalgic second best. As Foxglove grew up he might become, in effect, her father, teach her to recognize bird song, and destroy cats. He never remembered Sandra or Briony giving him a direct answer, but from now onwards the soft toys he brought the little girl began to be labelled, 'From your loving G.F.'

Back at Meadowsweet, on the evening Ernest made his proposal, Tiffany Boon was completing an application for a course in tropical hygiene, to fit herself for going to Ceylon – as she persisted in calling it – and caring for wounded Tamil Tigers.

That afternoon Joseph Cuff instructed six estate agents to put his house and meadow on the market. Bitterly, he told them to ask a price which was a sixth of what he might have received in compensation, even though it was twice what his villa had cost. He would buy a nice place in Golders Green. That should please her, though of course, she would never admit it.

Later the same evening as dusk fell Lorna Furnival stood at her garden window looking across her lawn to the trees which fringed it. She sipped her brandy and Horlicks and scowled. Away to her right in the garden room she could hear those foolish girls drooling over the child. Poor thing, it would grow up no happier than any other. All that fuss, all that silly hope. She was angry with the lot of them, but chiefly with herself for ever letting herself become angry. She was soon what Harry would have called squiffy.

The following Sunday morning the Revd Charles Sage preached before an unusually large congregation – twelve. He was in benevolent form. 'Let us give thanks to the Lord,' he began, 'that what He seemed about to take away He has generously given back.'

'The cheek of it!' Polly Langridge muttered. 'Claiming the credit for his blithering Lord! Who does he think he is?'

Next day Michael Ranch left 2 Keats Villas, where, unfortunately, the smell of rotting linoleum in the kitchen made him want to vomit, and went by coach to Harrogate to ask his wife, Virginia, who had tactlessly chosen the previous day to run away in earnest, and ask her to forgive him. To this she agreed, only telling him on the return journey that she was pregnant. She wasn't, but she intended to be.

Wendy Fisher meanwhile had told Fred that she was no longer pregnant. 'Too much excitement by half.' Fred was privately relieved. They consoled each other with an overpriced bottle of indifferent Burgundy, Fred as yet unaware of the new problem which was travelling south to confront him.

Soon afterwards Admiral and Lady Hawker called on their daughter, Briony, to tell her they had restored her allowance, and Briony gave her father a big hug.

'At least they didn't elope,' Anne told Jack as they hobbled home.

'Make a note of that,' Jack Hawker said. 'Take them some next time. Lifebuoy's the stuff. Matter of fact they smelt quite clean.'

During the next two weeks Mrs Volga made herself so tedious to the police that they traced Mr Taylor, and she travelled to Seaford to bring him home. The two of them then moved into Mr Taylor's house where they began to restore his garden. Though each found the other lovable, they played no erotic games with red watering-cans, as Fred Fisher hinted they did. Mr Taylor usually slept in his shed. 'To make sure it's not stolen,' Fred explained.

It was one dark autumn evening that Joan Wodge murdered Wilfred Wodge, using the long-handled brass warming pan which was the main ornament of the Red Lion's inglenook, and was sent to Holloway, where she became quite a favourite. All day she smiled at the warders, who looked forward to her release with sorrow.

As for Evan Mullins, he reopened his shop.

'Too late,' he would say, as he watched for little fingers pilfering chocolate bars, but not too late for him to discover an ironic pleasure in being nice to people. Besides, he was still alive, unlike another he could name. He soon became an institution and Polly Langridge encouraged people to patronize him.

Irma Svenson left Ralph Gamble and set up house with Keith Haresnip in Bognor Regis. There they were shagging each other stupid, as Fred Fisher reported, claiming to have secret information. They lived on the proceeds of an erotic

novel they had written together, Irma supplying the sex, Haresnip the prose. After five years, however, Irma returned to Sweden where she married a rich, middle-aged baron, but she and Haresnip continued to exchange affectionate letters, hers usually beginning, 'My dearest little English fucker.'

After she had gone, the focal point of Ralph Gamble's life became, as before, the winter pheasant slaughter. He didn't exclude the possibility of taking a new au pair. Dr Sweet assured him that one testicle was quite sufficient. But at 63 he was unwilling to take the risk. Anyway, how would he ever find another Irma?

Sir Rupert Brandish made sensible use of the abandonment of the Plan. 'I am delighted to confirm to the council,' he told its next meeting, 'that those of us who have always considered the introduction of an urban element into an Area which, if not yet declared to be of Outstanding Natural Beauty, would,' he promised, 'soon be so nominated.'

The architect of the Plan, far away in his London office of concrete and reflecting glass, was at first dismayed, but quickly became involved in a new project: the design of a concourse for a new town. At one end of this the church would, of course, have to be preserved, but at the other end, why not a pond large enough to be called a lake?

And in this – it came to him in an inspired flash – a colony of those visually fulfilling newts which had wrecked his last commission. The whole concourse might be called Newt Town. He was sure that enough of the creatures could easily be netted, and if they liked the nasty black sludge they'd previously inhabited, two or three tanker-loads would hardly cost a fortune and could easily be acquired. The architect had not yet met Lorna Furnival.

Some dozen years later Miss Wiggum – retired to a Dorset

cottage – returned to the village to become godmother to Justin Prone's first child. He had married Elsie Patch.

'We reckoned we ought have called her Thistledown, Miss Wiggum. Seeing that's what brought us together in a manner of speaking.'

What a pretty name. Miss Wiggum smiled benignly. She had long forgotten the playground outrage to which Justin referred.